Devilweed

Also by Bill Knox

DEVILWEED

Bill Knox

Constable • London

Constable & Robinson Ltd
3 The Lanchesters
162 Fulham Palace Road
London W6 9ER
www.constablerobinson.com

First published in Great Britain 1966
This edition published in Great Britain by Constable,
an imprint of Constable & Robinson Ltd 2008

ISBN: 978-1-84529-694-0

Printed and bound in the EU

Chapter One

H.M. Fishery Cruiser *Marlin* was in a hurry. She came out from the shelter of the Sound of Mull, took the first heavy seas of the open Minch beyond with a heave and roll of her slim grey shape, and continued on at the same hammering thirty-knot pace. The foaming wash from her twin screws marked a swing of course to almost due west while the same gusting wind which whip-cracked the blue Fishery Protection ensign at her stern sent spume drenching high along her decks.

It was a Wednesday morning in mid-October, a day of bright sunlight and scudding, wisping cloud. To the north, on the mainland, Ardnamurchan Point formed a crisp, rugged finger of land tipped with a white lighthouse tower. But neither mainland nor the islands beyond interested the men on the fishery cruiser's bridge deck.

'Freshening up again.' Chief Officer Webb Carrick made it both comment and question as another curtain of spray combed from *Marlin's* distinctive sharp-raked bow.

'I've noticed.' Captain Shannon glared past the helmsman who stood between them. 'Bothering you, Mr Carrick?'

Carrick stayed silent, caught a quick flicker of a grin of sympathy from the seaman, and slowly shook his head. The worst of the previous night's storm had blown itself out before dawn, and what was left was little more than a trailing remnant. Only an occasional floating patch of dark green wrack weed, torn loose from the sea bed, hinted at the violence which had passed.

Small and stout, with his bearded, moon-like face set in a peevish scowl, *Marlin's* skipper was in no mood for small talk. According to the patrol schedule he'd decided on so carefully over breakfast, his ship should have been heading north.

That was before the message which had crackled into the radio room a scant twenty minutes previously. Sometime during the night the lobster boat *Mora* had vanished from her moorings off Kenbeg Island. And now the lighthouse at Black Reef, some thirty sea-miles from their position, had reported sighting what looked like a boat drifting and out of control.

'Two points starboard.' Shannon waited until the helmsman, a gaunt-faced East Coaster, acknowledged the order, then judged the cruiser's next roll and used it to cross towards Carrick. 'You'd like me to ease up a bit, mister?'

'No, sir. I – well, I just wondered.' Webb Carrick left the rest unsaid. Shannon was senior captain in the Fishery Protection Squadron and *Marlin*, her 180-foot length built to cope with the worst Atlantic gale, needed no cosseting. Yet at the same time she drew a scant fathom and a half below the waterline. It was a vital need in off-shore patrol work, but the result was a vicious corkscrew roll when she was cramming on speed in any sort of broken sea.

'You wondered why the rush, eh?' Shannon gave a grunt. 'Look at your charts, mister. Kenbeg's the main island in the Rathbeg cluster – and that's fifteen miles to the north-west of Black Reef. It's open water, but if this boat off Black Reef is the *Mora* then she didn't get there on her own. To do that would be against tide, current, and every other damned thing I can think to name.'

From Shannon, it was a verdict which couldn't be questioned. The bearded sixty-year-old knew his coastal waters – and his fishermen – like few others.

'And if somebody took her out and is still aboard –'
Carrick gave a soft, appreciative whistle. Fishery
Protection files already held a fat bundle of letters, reports,
charges and countercharges concerning the Kenbeg lobster
fishers and their stubborn antagonism towards any outsiders who tried to operate in their area. They were pre-
pared to fend off any intruder who dared to work within
their self-declared domain – and more than a few of those
past intruders had the scars to prove that the Kenbeg
methods were seldom gentle. 'You think this could be the
start of more trouble?'

'If another Kenbeg boat finds her first, yes.' Shannon let
his ship slide back from another roll before he continued.
'The *Mora* belongs to a trouble-making old devil named
Sawny MacKenna. Half of the population of Kenbeg are
related to him in some way or other, and he acts as lord
high admiral as far as the local boats are concerned.'

'You know him, sir?' asked Carrick – and regretted it as
Shannon's face reddened to an angry hue.

'I know him – and he knows me,' said Shannon harshly.
He looked out across the heaving water with narrowed
eyes. 'The weather should settle down again before long.
I'm going down to my cabin. But call me when you sight
Black Reef – or that blasted boat.'

Carrick nodded, waited until the older man had walked
past the tiny chartroom at the rear of the bridge, then
relaxed a little as Shannon disappeared down the companionway stair. On the bulkhead beside the gyro
compass the roll indicator's pendulum took another
swing. Another, heavier drenching of spray battered
against the wheelhouse glass, and he heard the helmsman
give a chuckle of sympathy as it cleared to show an
oilskin-clad crewman making a quick scuttle across the
open foredeck.

For Carrick the scene was familiar enough. He'd been
two years with the Fishery Protection Service, ever since
an old, half-forgotten application had brought him a

sudden interview and an appointment as Chief Officer on *Marlin*, bringing with it the black-covered warrant card which assigned him the powers and pay of an assistant Superintendent of Fisheries. The appointment had come at a good time, just after he'd gained his deep-sea master's ticket only to discover there were plenty of similar young Merchant Navy officers with equal qualification – but not enough ships to go round.

The change had been startling at first, from bulky ocean-going tramps to the neat lines of *Marlin's* mere 400 tons. But he was Fishery Protection now, as near to a sea-going policeman as they came. And the fishery cruisers, small, grey destroyer-like craft but carrying no deck armament, bore a heavy responsibility. Their authority was their Blue Ensigns with the Fishery crest of gold anchor and thistle wreath, and it was their job to enforce the maze of regulations which governed Britain's multi-million-pound fishing industry. Dealing with as strongly independent a customer as the average fisherman, that wasn't easy.

Yet it was early for trouble to break, less than a day since they'd relieved their sister ship *Skua* on the Hebridean beat, that long scatter of islands which edged most of the north-west coast of Scotland. Five hundred islands, from uninhabited pimples of rock upwards, the Hebrides stretched 130 miles in length from tip to tail. To poets and painters they were islands of lonely romance. But to the watchdog fishery cruisers they were something else, a place of treacherous shoals, of dangerous channels and fierce tidal rips, all exposed to the full force of the open Atlantic. Now, for the next month, it was *Marlin's* task again to keep the peace around those shores – keep the peace and maintain the fishing laws in an area where a Fishery officer rated second only to tax collectors in terms of unpopularity.

Webb Carrick's broad-boned face split into a grin at the thought, and for the moment he looked even younger than his thirty-one years. Lips which were perhaps too thin and often left an impression of sardonic amusement backed the decisive character of the strong nose and dark brown eyes above. With a weather-bronzed skin and close-cut dark brown hair, his five foot ten of stocky build seemed made for the naval uniform he wore with thick-soled seaboots and white roll-necked sweater.

Beneath his feet, the wheelhouse mats vibrated with the throbbing drive of *Marlin's* diesels. Down below, he knew, her crew would be cursing those pitching decks, the drenching spray and the chance which had turned their leisurely prowl into this hammering dash. He glanced at the compass binnacle and then at the steering indicator and nodded to the helmsman. They were dead on course. Before long, they'd be able to pick up the Black Reef Lighthouse on the 25-mile radar scan – but before that happened, there were some things to arrange.

The bridge intercom was on the bulkhead panel behind him. He lifted the telephone piece, pressed the intercom's number four button, and waited until Jumbo Wills, *Marlin's* junior second mate, answered at the other end.

'Climb out of that bunk and come on up,' said Carrick briskly. 'I've got a job for you.'

'Eh?' The youngster groaned over the wire. *Marlin*, with a crew of twenty-four, normally carried three watchkeeping officers under Captain Shannon. But Wills's opposite number was ashore, giving evidence in an illegal trawling case – and the junior mate had little chance to rest.

'When do I sleep?' he protested.

'Later,' soothed Carrick. 'Bring the bo'sun with you. And the bridge watch could use some coffee.'

He hung up and was reaching into his jacket pocket for a cigarette when the hitherto silent helmsman gave a low murmur of interest.

'Look over there, sir – to port!'

'Nice – very nice.' Carrick drew a slow breath of appreciation as he saw for himself. Coming up from the south, the big cruising catamaran running a full-sail course

9

towards them was a marriage of all that was best in old and new. Her slim twin hulls joined by a glassed-over island bridge, the yacht had the wind almost directly astern of her – and was making the most of it. Three hundred square feet of crimson nylon spinnaker ballooned from her mast, straining her forward. The twin bows cut lightly through the raking seas, and the cat seemed almost rock-steady in her swift, taut-roped progress.

'That's all of twelve knots she's doing,' mused the helmsman.

'Somebody knows how to handle a sail,' agreed Carrick absently. He made a fast calculation and decided that the catamaran, a full eight-metre job by her size, would pass close astern of *Marlin* if both held their course and speed. The yacht's crew seemed to have reached the same conclusion and her track stayed constant.

Feet shuffled on the deck behind him, then Jumbo Wills's voice sounded in his ear, a note close to awe in the words. 'That's what I call real living, Webb. Now, if I had a boat like that –'

'You'd crew it with dolly-birds and head for the South Seas,' guessed Carrick cynically. 'But I wouldn't give odds on you getting there. She's fast all right – and that's a full fourteen-foot beam they're handling.'

Wills, plump and sandy-haired, helped himself to the bridge binoculars and focussed them on the big crimson spinnaker. Then he examined the yacht below with growing interest. 'Two aboard her. There's . . . yes, I think there's a boy steering her.'

'What name?'

'Eh?' Wills lowered the glasses and blinked.

'The boat, I mean,' said Carrick wearily. 'Here, give me them.'

He took the glasses, swore softly as *Marlin* pitched, then found and held the yacht in the powerful lenses. Her superstructure was white, but the twin hulls were in a crimson which colour-matched that vast, swelling spinnaker. Spume blurred around the boat as he tried to read her name.

'*Coosh* . . . no, *Gooshgash*. Well, I suppose it means something –' He shrugged and continued the examination. Every inch of the cat's deck and rigging showed fresh and clean, telling of hours of attention. On the bridge island, behind the tabernacle-stepped mast, two figures were plainly visible. One was a man, probably about his own age, dressed in oilskins and with a knitted wool cap on his head. The other figure . . . Carrick studied it for a moment and gave a chuckle of approval.

'Jumbo –'

'What?'

'Your boy's a girl.'

She was standing on the port side, almost certainly at the wheel which would control the catamaran's big twin rudders. He could make out short, dark hair, a heart-shaped face and a slim but far from boyish figure which a lightweight crimson sailing jacket did little to obscure. The rest – he saw her turn, as if speaking to her companion and laughing. He had a spray-fogged impression of high cheekbones and a wide, generous mouth, then lowered the binoculars with a reluctant sigh.

'Well?' queried Wills impatiently.

'She's a girl all right,' confirmed Carrick. 'Where's the coffee?'

'Bo'sun's bringing it.' Wills gave a soft whistle as he caught sight of the engine rev. counter's reading. 'Hey, cramming it on a bit, aren't we?'

'Tell the skipper,' suggested Carrick dryly.

'Oh.' The topic died then and there as far as the youngster was concerned. Then he brightened. 'Hey, the cat's signalling.'

They watched the light which blinked from the yacht, its Morse ragged but readable.

Carrick chuckled as the message ended. '"Where's the

fire?" – well, when they hit our wash they're not going to be so friendly.'

'Will I answer?' queried Wills.

'No. Just give 'em a wave.'

Jumbo Wills waved enthusiastically. Then, as the yacht began to fall astern, Carrick called him back to the task at hand. 'Jumbo, I want you to take radar watch –' He broke off as a burly figure squeezed along the companionway into the bridge, a flask of coffee under one arm, a nest of cups cradled in his hands. Petty Officer William 'Clapper' Bell, *Marlin's* bo'sun, six feet of muscular Glasgow-Irishman, beamed around him.

'Is there a job on, sir?' His voice was a hoarse and hopeful boom.

Carrick nodded. 'There's a fishing boat adrift near Black Reef. If there's anyone aboard, he won't necessarily welcome us.'

The bo'sun smacked his lips. 'Fair enough.'

'I want the launch checked and readied for lowering, with a couple of men standing by. Later on we'll need bridge lookouts port and starboard. You'll come with me on the launch.' Carrick turned towards Wills. 'Jumbo, you'd better get the radio room to call up Black Reef light and ask if they've anything fresh to tell us.'

'Will do.' The second mate raised a questioning eyebrow. 'Any idea whose boat it is, Webb?'

'The *Mora* – belongs to a lobsterman named MacKenna, according to the Old Man.'

'That she does!' Clapper Bell gave a snort of mixed delight and surprise. 'Last time he and the captain met up was three years ago. We caught MacKenna red-handed doing a spot of inshore poaching, but then the cunning old goat made the captain –' He remembered the helmsman, and stopped short. 'Well, let's just say it's a small world, sir. Far too small when the pair of them meet up!'

'Which means happy days are here again.' Carrick grimaced, then glanced astern. The catamaran was just clearing the broken white of their wash. The girl aboard must have had a hectic few moments while it had lasted.

'How about that coffee?' queried Wills.

Clapper Bell spread the cups on the bridge table, uncorked the vacuum flask, and sniffed happily at its contents.

'Galley coffee?' A twist of a smile touched Carrick's mouth as he observed what was almost a ritual.

'Aye – but with the usual wee fortification,' said the bo'sun, winking. Just where he hid the bottle was one of the privileges of being the fishery cruiser's senior P.O.

Inevitably, Captain Shannon's weather forecast was correct. By 0940 hours, when they first picked up Black Reef Lighthouse on the radar screen, the sea was already moderating. Thirty minutes later, when the slim lighthouse tower was at about ten miles range, the wind was little more than a gentle breeze and the waves had dropped to a slow, gentle swell. Carrick checked that the lookouts were at their posts, one man on each of the open bridge wings, then buzzed Captain Shannon's cabin on the intercom.

Shannon came up at once. He heaved himself up into his command chair behind the helmsman, settled back with a grunt and looked around him.

'What's the situation, mister?'

Carrick shook his head. The last report from the lighthouse hadn't been helpful. 'Black Reef say they've lost sight of the boat, sir. She drifted beyond their vision limit.'

'Huh.' Shannon digested the information with a pained expression. 'What was the last bearing they had?'

'Due north-west.' Carrick waited. The lighthouse tower was a growing white speck in the open sea ahead. A deceptively thin line of breaking surf around its base told of the rocks it guarded.

13

'Very well.' Shannon gave a sigh. 'Alter course to north-west and reduce speed to twelve knots. We'll commence visual and radar search, but hold your radar to the two-mile scan. Bo'sun –'

'Sir?' Clapper Bell crossed to his side.

'Make sure these lookouts keep their eyes open. They know what we're trying to find?'

'I've told them, sir.' Bell hesitated, his rugged face puzzled. 'I remember the *Mora*, sir. She's only an old sixteen-footer with an inboard engine. Who'd want to steal a tub like that?'

'Steal?' Shannon made the word nearly a snarl. 'That's one choice. Maybe it's the likeliest – but for all I know MacKenna could have towed the thing out and tried to sink it for the insurance money. With him, anything's possible.'

Their first sweep drew a blank. Searching for a larger craft would have been a fairly simple operation, a matter of watching for any intruding blip on *Marlin's* radar. But, like most of her kind, the missing lobster boat was too small, too low in the water to be picked up except at close range. The cruiser ploughed on until at last Shannon ordered a ninety-degree turn to port. He held her on the new course for a full ten minutes then made a second ninety-degree turn, sending *Marlin* running parallel to her original track.

The starboard lookout was first to spot the vague shape rolling low and listlessly in the steel-blue water. The *Marlin's* engines slowed in obedience to a fresh clamour of telegraph signals from her bridge, and she approached the hulk ahead at little more than a crawl, diesel exhaust purring quietly from her squat funnel. But there was something wrong, very wrong. Carrick sensed it from the sudden set of Captain Shannon's mouth as the older man lowered the bridge glasses from his eyes.

'Here –' Shannon passed them over.

The twin images cleared as Carrick refocussed. Captain Shannon's eyes were no longer as keen as they once had been.

'Well?'

'Cabin cruiser – and her deck's awash. No sign of life.' Carrick took his time, conscious of a strange, raw tension behind the skipper's impatience. The boat ahead was barely afloat, each low wave rolling lazily over her length. 'I'd say she's a forty-footer, anything up to ten tons.' There was a small radio mast set above the cabin cruiser's wheelhouse cockpit, a pram dinghy was still lashed to the deck near her bow, and a long streamer of dark brown seaweed washed lazily around her flooded bow hatchway. Devilweed was the name fishermen gave it – that long brown algae with its frayed, leathery fronds was seldom seen on the surface unless a storm had passed.

Suddenly he understood Shannon's tension. In the intervals between waves he had an occasional glimpse of her hull, a white hull with a distinctive red and green chequered band running its length just below deck level.

'You know her, mister?' demanded Shannon.

Carrick took a deep breath. 'She's the *Thrift*, sir.'

They'd come looking for a lobster boat. Instead, they'd run straight into what, for Captain Shannon, could be personal tragedy.

For nearly a year the *Thrift* had been the pride of the Bank of Central Scotland, their unique floating branch, the marine bank which served the islands. From Stornoway in the north right down to Barra in the south, the specially fitted cabin cruiser had brought the blessings of chequebooks and savings accounts, loans and mortgages and all the other ammunition of modern banking to the islanders' doorstep. And one of her crew, a junior clerk, was Shannon's nephew.

'There should be three men aboard her.' Shannon's voice held a cracked edge, and the other men on the bridge avoided his gaze. He chewed hard on his lower lip for a moment. 'My – I know they fitted her with extra buoyance chambers, lifeboat style, for this bank boat job.'

'And that looks about all that's keeping her afloat,' muttered Clapper Bell softly.

If Shannon heard him, he gave no sign. He sat where he was for a long moment, silent. Then, at last, he climbed down from his chair. 'Carrick, you and the bo'sun get into those frogman rigs you're always so keen to use. Find out if – well, if there's any sign of what happened and how badly she's damaged. But don't risk your necks . . . understood?'

With *Marlin* hove to on the weather side of the waterlogged cabin cruiser, her launch cut a fast course towards the half-submerged bank boat. As they travelled, Webb Carrick finished fastening the zip cuffs of his black neoprene rubber 'wet' suit and waited while Clapper Bell did the same to his own outfit. The lightweight 'wet' suits didn't keep a diver dry, but trapped a thin layer of water between suit and diver, building up its own heat from the wearer's body. The air cylinders and other scuba gear lay at their feet, ready for use.

They eyed the *Thrift* with sober care as the gap closed and their craft throbbed round in a close-range inspection. But there was no visible damage to the bank boat and still no sign of life or death.

'Edge alongside,' Carrick told the man at the helm. 'Take it gently . . . as gently as you can.' He turned to Bell. 'Clapper, get on your gear and check the hull. I'll see what she's like deck-side.'

By the time the launch's side fenders kissed against the bank boat's hull both men were ready. Clapper Bell pulled his glass face-mask into position, double-checked his air supply, nodded, and eased himself into the water. As his head disappeared and a thin trail of air bubbles began rising, Carrick made his own move. The aqualung ready on his back but his face-mask still raised, he swung himself across the narrow gap between the two boats and splashed down into the *Thrift's* sea-washed deck. From there, moving clumsily, the frogman gear still out of its element and its weight slowing him, he crossed the slightly canting deck to the cockpit. Behind him he could hear the gentle throb of the launch engine. But on the cabin cruiser there was no sound except the wash of the waves, the gentle bumping of loose fitments somewhere below and an occasional creak from her hull.

There was about three feet of water in the cockpit. He lowered himself in and began a methodical inspection while tiny wavelets lapped against his thighs.

On the control panel the engine throttles were closed and the gear lever set at neutral. The gentle swing of a cupboard door, moving to and fro in the swirling water, caught his attention. He went over, opened it, and gave a low whistle of surprise. The cupboard held the *Thrift's* radio – and the transmitter had been wrecked, smashed by more than one heavy blow.

Carrick made another splashing tour of the cockpit. On the navigation table, a water-soaked chart was still spread out, held in place by two spring-clips. He peered down at it, then paused as he heard a movement on the upper deck. A moment later Clapper Bell dropped down beside him, face-mask shoved back, his breathing tube hanging free, water dripping from his suit.

'Not a dam' thing wrong wi' her underside that I can find.' The bo'sun's frown deepened. 'You don't look surprised –' He stopped short as Carrick pointed silently to the wrecked transmitter, then, as he saw for himself, gave a growl. 'Hell, if this means what I think, we've really found trouble, sir.'

Carrick nodded. Ashore, the phrase was bank robbery. But at sea there was another, an older word – piracy. The *Thrift* would have been an easy enough capture, and it was more than unlikely that she'd carried any special security equipment. Even on shore, Scottish banks took remarkably few precautions against raiders. Bank guards were found in only a few main offices and aboard cash delivery trucks operating in cities. At night, many a bank branch had no burglar alarm system in operation. Scottish bankers had an almost child-like faith in the impregnability of their strongrooms.

He sighed. 'Clapper, where would you expect to find the seacocks on a thing this size?'

'Probably under the bilges in the main saloon.' The bo'sun scrubbed one hand across his mouth. 'That's the bankin' area, wi' the livin' quarters aft. I'd a look over her once at Stornoway – the Old Man sent me aboard wi' a letter for his nephew. A pretty decent young bloke, that one.'

'Where was the safe?'

'Eh . . . set centre in the saloon.' Bell knew what was coming next, and didn't like it. 'Look, sir, it's likely to be as black as the Earl o' Hell's waistcoat down there. An' if she starts slidin' . . .'

'Then I'll come out a lot faster than I went in.' Carrick shook his head. 'If she was going to sink she'd have done it by now, Clapper. Anyway, I'm not going to try anything spectacular. Just in and out.'

The bo'sun shrugged. 'You're the boss. But I don't fancy goin' back aboard *Marlin* on my own.'

Carrick gave a brief grin, pulled down his face-mask, gripped the scuba's breathing tube between his teeth, and crossed to where the top of the saloon companionway stair was just visible above the water. He opened the scuba's regulator valve then, one hand on each of the stairway rails, made his way down until the water was chest deep. He felt the chill as the wet suit filled, then let himself sink under.

Clapper Bell's forecast had been fairly close to truth – moving inside the saloon was like swimming in a dark green velvet fog, with only a faint glimmer of light penetrating from the submerged portholes. He collided with a

18

floating chair, brushed through a cloud of eerily clinging papers and, working his way on, banged into something more solid. His fingers caught and held an upright metal grille. The bank counter, he guessed. Dropping lower, he found deck level and worked back along the cabin until the black bulk of the safe appeared inches ahead. He worked round to the door, found it closed, and tugged hard on the massive brass handle. It didn't move. He tried again, harder, with the same negative result and sat back on his haunches for a moment trying to make sense of the fact.

Another task remained. He searched along the decking until he found what he'd anticipated, the place where an oblong section of plank had been removed. He turned his body, bubbles trailing from the scuba's exhaust valve, and groped shoulder-deep into the hole. The hard shape of a seacock tap met his fingers – and the tap was open.

Carrick headed towards the companionway, hauled himself up the short flight of steps, and came back into the light and air of the cockpit. Clapper Bell was still there, the same frown on his rugged, leathery face.

'Find what you wanted?' he asked once Carrick had shed the scuba mask.

Carrick took a deep breath, then another, and nodded. 'Seacocks are open – but the safe is closed.'

'You mean it wasn't a hold-up?'

'I don't know.' Carrick levered himself up on the cockpit rim. 'We'll take a look aft, Clapper. Then we'll signal to *Marlin*. We'll need some help before she's fit to tow.'

'To tow?' Petty Officer Bell gave a sniff of doubt. 'Well, no harm in tryin', I suppose. Eh . . . the three blokes who were on board, sir. Did you . . .?'

Carrick shook his head. 'No. But if the living quarters were aft then we'd better make sure.'

The three tiny cabins near the stern were a chaos of drifting clothes and bedding but held nothing more. As for

19

what had happened – once *Marlin* received their signal, there was too much work to be done to leave any time for thought. It took two hours of sheer physical effort before they could be sure that the one-time cabin cruiser was secure, two hours during which they spent most of their time inside her hull.

First came half-a-dozen suitcase-like collapsible life rafts, ferried over from the fishery cruiser. They packed them at strategic intervals below *Thrift's* deck then triggered the little CO_2 bottles attached to each. The rubber rafts swelled to life, adding their buoyancy to the vessel.

When that was done, they surfaced, changed air cylinders aboard their launch, and took time for a breather and a cigarette.

One thing at least was certain. The *Thrift* was already riding easier in the water.

'We've got a visitor comin'.' Clapper Bell nudged Carrick and gave a jerk of his head. Another boat was on its way across from the fishery cruiser.

Carrick took a last draw on his cigarette, tossed the stub into the water, and looked round. He gave a wry grimace. Captain Shannon was in the sternsheets of the other boat – and a couple of minutes later he stepped aboard their launch with a curt nod of greeting.

'I've radioed a full report to shore,' he said shortly. 'It's causing one devil of a commotion. You're sure the safe is still locked?'

'As sure as I can be.' Webb Carrick felt a twinge of irritation. Did Shannon expect him to have humped the thing out on his back?

Shannon hardly waited for an answer. 'Let's hope you're right. There should be close on fifty thousand pounds inside that damned box. Only bank staff knew the figure.'

'Fifty thousand –' Carrick showed his surprise.

'Special run,' said Shannon grimly. 'I've had the details via Oban Radio. The *Thrift* left Oban two days ago, and was working her way up towards Uist. That's routine –

but this was also the once-a-month trip when she took money packages to two or three branches on the bigger islands – the rest of the cash was because there's a cattle sale due in Uist this week and cattle dealers like cash on the barrel.'

'And the crew, sir?' asked Clapper Bell awkwardly.

Shannon's face tightened. 'The usual. Henderson their regular coxswain-engineer, Wilson the manager, and young Andrew . . . Andrew Sword the clerk.' The bearded mouth closed for a moment and he acknowledged their murmur of sympathy with a nod. 'Seems they left Iona at mid-afternoon yesterday. Their idea was to press on to the next island on their list, lie up there overnight, and be open for business first thing this morning.'

'And the next island?' asked Carrick.

'Kenbeg.' Shannon almost snarled the name. 'Last night's storm probably changed their plans, but don't ask me how the rest fits, mister. We go out looking for one boat that disappears from Kenbeg – and find another that damn well never got there.'

And with the crew missing, Carrick nearly added. But he saw the raw hurt in the older man's eyes and instead swung himself on to the gunwale of the launch. 'We'll be ready to receive a tow line soon, sir,' he promised. 'Bo'sun –'

Clapper Bell gave a quick, thankful nod and settled his face-mask back in position.

The last stage of the job, closing the seacocks, was a cramped, fumbling, knuckle-barking process. There were three to be dealt with, two in the saloon and the third aft, behind the crew quarters – the latter jammed tight and hard, as if it would never move. Sweating in their suits, struggling clumsily in the close-range glare of a diving lamp, they were near to exhaustion when the rusted metal finally freed. But when it did, Carrick knew a moment of weary triumph. Now the *Thrift* was ready to be towed – and if they could get her to where she could be beached in shallow water then low tide and a sound hull would allow her to be pumped dry.

Or would it? One thing more would have to be checked. He gripped Clapper Bell by the shoulder, signalled, and they flippered their way along the narrow companionway to the bank boat's engineroom. A tiny, frightened fish sped clear of their path, then the portable light shone on a new problem.

The door to the engineroom was little more than an oblong hatch, too small to allow a man with an aqualung to squeeze through. They hand-signalled, then went into a drill they'd practised often enough, though usually in the less hazardous conditions of a Royal Naval Establishment test tank.

Carrick took a long, deep breath of air through the scuba tube, then released tube and the aqualung harness. While Clapper Bell held them ready, he squeezed through the doorway, took the aqualung as it was passed through after him, and slipped it on again. He cleared the mouthpiece with a bubbling gush of air from the tanks, slipped it into position, and blew the remaining water in the tubes out through the exhaust valve.

Clapper Bell's round face-mask still peered towards him from the doorway. He gave him a thumbs-up signal, took the portable light, and took less than a minute to find what he'd suspected. The sea-water inlet pipe to the engine's cooling jacket had been smashed loose – as effective an act as punching a hole through the *Thrift's* hull. The only thing he could do was plug the piping. He found a box of what had once been cleaning rags and rammed handful after handful of the stuff into the hole until it was packed close to solid.

He had to repeat the same drill with the aqualung to get out again. Then, twin streams of bubbles rising above them, the two men made their way back, climbed to the open air of the deck level above, and thankfully boarded the waiting launch.

22

Captain Shannon hadn't been idle. *Marlin* already had a tow line running from her stern to the bank boat's forepeak. As soon as their launch had been swung back aboard, the fishery cruiser's diesels began purring. Slowly, steadily, she moved ahead and the long manilla line rose dripping from the water to take the strain. At little more than four knots the tow began.

Jumbo Wills saw the launch secured, then turned to help Carrick and Clapper Bell strip off their gear.

'So the safe is still locked?' The young second mate scratched his head. 'Then how the heck can it be robbery? Unless . . . unless the three blokes aboard decided to do a vanishing trick and took the money with them. That's just the sort of thing those bank boys would do – take the cash, then lock up as they leave.'

'Better not let the Old Man hear you on that tack,' warned Clapper Bell, peeling out of his rubber suit and rough-towelling his hairy frame.

'There's no sense in it anyway.' His own suit discarded, Carrick shivered a little as he rubbed himself down. 'They'd know *Thrift* had extra buoyancy tanks. Somebody – an outsider – tried to scuttle her without realizing just what he was up against. And whoever he was, he couldn't wait around to see the job done.' He finished, and wrapped the damp towel round his middle. 'Look, Jumbo, she's still carrying her dinghy. In this nice neat theory of yours what did her crew do? Swim ashore?'

The second mate shrugged and looked back at the cabin cruiser, wallowing sluggishly along at the end of *Marlin's* hawser. 'Well, I'd still like to be around when that safe is opened.'

'Did the skipper say where we were heading?' asked Carrick.

'Kenbeg Island.' Wills flushed a little. 'He says it's the nearest harbour with a good beaching area. I suggested Barra – and got told to mind my own business.'

23

'Mister, I'd do just that,' advised Carrick soberly. He left Wills standing open-mouthed and went below.

In the quiet of his cabin, changing back into uniform, he thought again of Shannon. There was too much worry gnawing inside *Marlin's* captain for him to take kindly to unwanted advice. Yet Jumbo Wills was right on one point – when that safe was opened, whether the money was there or not, a whole fresh set of questions would demand answers.

The black intercom telephone above his bunk buzzed as he pulled on a fresh shirt. He swore mildly, then lifted the receiver.

A familiar spikey voice crackled frigidly in his ear. 'Whatever you may imagine, mister, you haven't qualified for a rest cure. This is still your duty watch.'

Webb Carrick grimaced at the mouthpiece.

'I'm on my way now, sir,' he promised.

Chapter Two

At that plodding four-knot pace and with the wind freshening, it was mid-afternoon before *Marlin* neared her destination. Twice she spotted fishing boats. The first were a group of dark-hulled seine netters, the basket signals at each masthead showing gear was down and crews hard at work. The second sighting was different, a single lobster boat, small and narrow, two men aboard, engine thumping purposefully as she steered towards the fishery cruiser.

Electric loud-hailer and old-style bull horn bellowed across the intervening stretch of water. She was a Kenbeg boat, the fishermen agreed, staring with undisguised curiosity at the wallowing cabin cruiser under tow. Yes, they were out helping to search for the missing *Mora* – but so far they'd drawn a blank.

And Sawny MacKenna?

'He's ashore now at Kenbeg,' rasped the bull horn. 'But he was out at dawn this morning trying to find some trace of her.'

They exchanged friendly-enough salutes, then the lobster boat turned busily away towards the south-west while *Marlin* continued on course. Before long, the Rathbeg Isles began to loom ahead, standing out of the sea like a scatter of rocky fragments. It was as if this trio of islands had somehow come adrift from the rest of the Hebridean chain, to be deposited in chance and not particularly happy isolation.

Kenbeg, the largest, about two miles across by little more than a mile and a half in length, showed on the Admiralty chart like a dog's head with the mouth opened wide to the east to form a natural haven for small craft. Near the mouth, as if it were a steak about to be eaten, sat Buidhe – the name meant golden in the old Gaelic tongue. Third and last, to the west, separated from Kenbeg by half a mile of open water, was Dearg, little more than a long narrow finger of wave-worn, spray-swept rock and shingle.

Dearg was low and useless, except to the grey seals which made it their home. Kenbeg's harbour bay, with its cluster of houses and narrow pier, was edged with sand and shingle, and though the rest of its coast was formed of high black basalt cliffs, the land surface was rich grazing for cattle and sheep. Lobster fishing might represent the main industry of the thirty or so families who lived on Kenbeg, but their animals formed a profitable second string.

Buidhe was different again, a sheltered place of gentle slopes. To the south, a wide deep-water channel separated it from Kenbeg's harbour bay – but near its northern tip the water was shallow enough to allow a man to walk from one island to the other at low tide. That, at least, was what the chart said. The most striking feature of Buidhe, as far as *Marlin's* crew were concerned, was the way the pale sunlight glinted on seemingly endless stretches of glass as the fishery cruiser steered up the buoyed south channel, close to the little island's shore.

'What the heck is that?' demanded Jumbo Wills. It was the second mate's bridge watch but Carrick as Chief Officer had stayed with him for the mooring operation. They'd seen little of Captain Shannon – he was spending most of his time closeted in the radio room.

'The glasswork?' Carrick eyed the spectacle with equal interest. 'Greenhouses – some patent medicine king named Tenford bought Buidhe lock, stock, and barrel about ten years back when he retired, then started a bulb-growing operation. They grow tulips, daffodils, that sort of thing.'

Wills blinked. 'I thought you hadn't been here before.'

'I haven't,' confessed Carrick. 'But I've heard about the place. They sell flowers to the mainland in the summer, but the bulbs are what they're really after. There's a lot of outside planting – the greenhouses are for forcing other stuff on.'

'And this character Tenford? Does he live on Buidhe?'

'He's dead now. But the bulb business has kept going.'

'Aye, and it's good soil they've got, sir,' volunteered their helmsman. 'I remember coming in here once in early summer – and that whole island was a mass of flowers in bloom. Like its name, it was a real golden isle.'

'Then let's not ram it,' advised Carrick mildly. 'Better watch those buoys.'

The helmsman grinned, but swung his wheel a point to port, shading them back into mid-channel.

They were tying up alongside the pier, an operation watched by a small and silent audience of young children and old fishermen, when Captain Shannon finally stumped out of the radio room.

'I'm going ashore,' he said abruptly. 'Mr Wills, you'll take a party of men and the launch – I want the *Thrift* beached on the other side of this bay, as far away from the village as you can make it. Make sure she's lying on as soft a bottom as possible and properly secured, then come back aboard. Mr Carrick –'

'Sir?'

'I'll need you later, so be ready.' He glanced back at Jumbo Wills. 'Waiting on something?'

'No . . . nothing, sir.' The second mate hustled off.

Shannon sighed and pulled thoughtfully at his beard. Then, without another word, he left the bridge. A moment later Carrick saw him march down the newly secured gangway and head off down the pier towards the village. Carrick relaxed, released the helmsman for a meal, used

27

the intercom to pass the same word down to the engine-room, then lit a cigarette and took his first real glance around.

Kenbeg was the duplicate of any number of other tiny Hebridean fishing villages. The cottages were small and low, built of white-washed stone and roofed in hand-split slate. Peat smoke drifted lazily from their chimneys. On the pier, several score of large black-backed gulls preened themselves among the waiting piles of lobster creels – not the wicker pots used in most parts of the world but the solid-based wood-hooped West Highland variety, each with its surrounding veil of dark-tanned herring net.

There were four boats lying in the bay. Three were lobster fishers, bright with paint, all around the sixteen-foot class with open deck, a covered inboard engine and a small stump mast which could carry a lug-sail if needed. The remaining boat was twice their size, a dull, elderly, sea-worn drifter with deckhouse and fish hatches, a radio aerial slung between her masts, her name painted over and only her fishing register number remaining. Carrick guessed her to be a prawn fisher, and wondered at her lying in a place where any but the local lobster boats were seldom welcome.

'Picture postcard stuff,' said the man in grimy blue overalls who edged up quietly beside him, leaning his elbows on the bridge wing. Andy Shaw, *Marlin's* chief engineer, was middle-aged, unshaven, and a seldom visitor into raw daylight.

'Most of their boats seem to be out,' said Carrick, thumbing towards the string of vacant, bobbing mooring cans which lay close to their berth.

'Looking for the one that got away?' Shaw chuckled. 'There used to be a fleet of about a dozen working from here.' Then he gave a grunt of new interest. 'Now that's what I call different, very different indeed. Over there, Webb, coming up-channel!'

28

It was the crimson catamaran. Sails lowered, she came in at a slow, leisurely pace with a trio of gulls forming a circling escort. A light haze of exhaust smoke rose from her soft-noted outboard engine, centre-mounted between the twin hulls. As they watched, the yacht crept the rest of the way towards the most distant of the mooring buoys. A slim figure moved swiftly along her deck, knelt ready and then scooped the can aboard with a swift and sure arm-movement.

Marlin's chief engineer blinked. 'That's a girl –'

'And she knows her boats,' agreed Carrick. 'We saw her this morning, on the way to Black Reef.'

'Aye. Well, at my age you prefer beer.' Shaw rubbed a set of oily fingers along his chin. 'Now look, Webb, I need to know what's happening next. First the Old Man wants maximum revs, then we're crawling along like a hearse on its way to a funeral! There's a wee job I'd like to do to the starboard diesel – but not if Shannon's going to have us chasing out of here before long.'

'Don't ask me,' said Carrick, shaking his head. 'Maybe when he comes back . . .'

'Aye, I'll have a word with him,' said Shaw. 'This is his ship, I'm not denying it. But they're my engines, though it's damned seldom he has the courtesy to remember.' He went away, still muttering to himself.

Carrick watched the catamaran for a moment or two longer, then as the girl disappeared from the deck and into its cabin he turned his attention to the activity at *Marlin's* stern. Jumbo Wills had the launch in the water and was taking the bank boat's towing line aboard. The tide was in and would soon be on the turn – which meant all the second mate had to do was to beach the *Thrift* as he'd been ordered. Low tide would leave her high and dry, ready to be pumped out.

He finished his cigarette and tossed the glowing stub overboard, where it sizzled to a sudden death in the lapping water. A gull lanced down to investigate, but barely touched the water before it rose again with a raucous squawk of disgust.

Life seemed a peaceful-enough idyll on Kenbeg Island. But he wondered how long it would stay that way.

Captain Shannon returned aboard in less than half an hour and brought a stranger with him. The new arrival was a tall, elderly fisherman with a mop of white, untamed hair, his thin frame clothed in dark jersey and grey corduroy trousers, his feet snug in a pair of worn plimsolls. Within moments of their arrival, a messenger summoned Carrick to the captain's day-cabin, set just below the bridge.

Shannon kept the formalities to a scowling minimum. 'This is MacKenna, the owner of the *Mora* – my Chief Officer, Mr Carrick.'

'Alexander MacKenna, but, och, most folk know me best as Sawny,' said the fisherman in a mild-enough manner, rising from his chair and extending one lean hand. Carrick guessed him to be in his mid-sixties. His grip was light but firm, his face wind-burned to the shade of well-oiled teak and showing a light stubble of beard around a long, whimsical jaw.

'I've heard of you, Mr MacKenna,' said Carrick.

'Aye, you probably will,' admitted MacKenna, in the same easy, soft-tongued fashion. 'There's a tale or two over the years. But I've been saying to Captain Shannon how sorry I am about this business of the *Thrift*. A bad business, Chief Officer, worse even than my own troubles.' He flickered a cautious sidelong glance at Shannon.

'Being sanctimonious isn't going to help,' exploded *Marlin's* skipper. His fist thumped down on the cabin table. 'If I ever want sympathy, I won't come looking in your direction. What I want is something you're less likely to stock – the truth.'

'But Captain –'

'Be quiet!' It came as almost a bellow. 'I warn you, MacKenna, I'm in no mood to waste time. Mr Carrick –'

'Sir?' Carrick looked from one man to the other, baffled.

'When was the *Mora* supposed to have disappeared from her moorings?'

'Last night some time, but –'

'Last night.' Shannon's voice became like crushed ice. 'Last night was Tuesday. Now then, MacKenna, let's have it in front of a witness. When did you first know the *Mora* was missing?'

MacKenna gnawed his lower lip. 'Well . . .'

'When?'

'Ach, the night before – Monday night. But I thought that someone had just borrowed it. Only, if he had, he'd have been back by last night.' The fisherman turned to Carrick, seeking either support or understanding. 'There's a lad on the island, Drammy MacPherson we call him. He often gives me a hand with the lobster fishing, so I let him take the *Mora* out on his own the odd time.'

'Huh.' Captain Shannon scowled across the table. 'And how much of this would you have told if I hadn't been grabbed by MacPherson's mother as soon as I reached the pier-end?'

'But I still don't know for sure that Drammy was on the *Mora*,' protested MacKenna with a spark of indignation. 'Listen, man, I was off the island on Monday night. When I got back and found the boat gone I thought he'd taken her – it was only when the *Mora* didn't show up yesterday that I began to worry. And then what was I to do?'

'Why not tell the truth?' snapped Shannon. 'Or would that be too much for your corkscrew mind?'

Carrick took a hand before the two antagonists came to blows. 'Mr MacKenna –'

'Sawny,' corrected the fisherman hopefully.

'All right, Sawny. Who saw MacPherson last?'

MacKenna ran one hand unhappily through his white hair. 'His mother. All she knows is that he drank the best

31

part of a bottle of the hard stuff on Monday night and then went wandering off on his own. He might have walked off a cliff for all I know – and in case you're wondering, we've already had a look along the shore.'

'If MacPherson didn't take the *Mora*, who else would?' probed Carrick.

MacKenna's eyes narrowed. 'An outsider might have done it. Maybe somebody from one o' the mainland lobster boats, the big poaching devils who're snatching our livelihood from under our noses.'

'Back to that . . .' Captain Shannon gave a weary shake of his head. 'You've been told before, MacKenna, you've no special territorial rights.'

'And I'll tell you,' growled his adversary, 'you may be a Superintendent of Fisheries or any other fancy title – but we'll fight for what's our own any way we need.'

'What about the *Thrift*?' asked Carrick suddenly. 'Did you know she'd be here today?'

'The bank boat?' MacKenna gave all the appearance of being taken aback. 'Aye, but – now see here, whatever happened it wasn't any Kenbeg man who tried to sink her!'

'Sink?' Captain Shannon's beard bristled. 'Who gave you that idea?'

For a moment MacKenna kept an uneasy silence. Then he shrugged. 'You've been using your radio, Captain. I've been listening to mine. Two messages you send, then there's a silence. But when I switch from the emergency wave length to another – and that's no crime – all I can hear is code signals flying back and forward between you and the shore.'

'Then answer me something else,' said Shannon softly. 'Where were you last night?'

Sawny MacKenna rose from his chair with a sudden, formal dignity. 'That, Captain Shannon, is none of your damn business.'

The two men glared at each other in silence for a long

minute. Then Shannon let out a slow, sighing breath. 'We'll see. That's all for now, MacKenna.'

The fisherman gave a brief nod and left them. Captain Shannon waited until the door had clicked shut then slumped back in his chair. 'Well, what do you make of him, Webb?'

Carrick felt a danger signal click into place at the use of his first name. 'He's quite a character – and something's making him far from happy.'

'Happy?' Shannon grunted. 'There's a bottle and glasses in my locker. Get them out, will you?'

The bottle was a twenty-year-old single blend malt whisky, one hundred per cent reserved for export. Carrick poured a stiff measure for Shannon, saw the unchanged expression on the bearded face, and added another inch of the golden liquid. He handed the drink over, and helped himself to a smaller tot.

'Good luck.' Shannon took a long swallow, coughed, and nursed the half-emptied glass between his fingers. 'You're going to need some, mister. I'm putting you ashore.'

'Here?' Carrick stopped with the whisky barely moistening his lips. 'Why?'

'Two reasons.' Shannon relaxed a little as the whisky warmed through him. 'These code signals MacKenna talked about are one. The nearest civilian policeman is a village cop half-a-dozen islands away. So Inverness County are flying two detectives over to Barra airstrip late tonight, and a Bank of Central Scotland man will come with them to open the *Thrift's* safe. I've to collect them on arrival at Barra and bring them here. We'll make a landing at Black Reef light on the way, to see what sense we can get out of the lighthouse keepers. While we're gone, somebody's got to keep an eye on things here.'

'When do you expect to be back?' asked Carrick. The idea of being marooned on Kenbeg for a spell held few attractions.

'Tomorrow, early afternoon – it depends on what happens.' Shannon took a more leisurely sip at his drink. 'Anyway, I'll leave you Petty Officer Bell, two ratings, and the rubber pack-boat. Officially, your job is to keep a guard on the *Thrift*, get her pumped dry and refloated if possible.'

'And unofficially?' Carrick had already guessed the rest.

'Find out what you can, where you can,' growled Shannon. 'Sawny MacKenna knows something, you've said as much yourself. It might be a link between his boat and the *Thrift*, it might not, but either way you probably won't get much help from the Kenbeg people, unless Drammy MacPherson's mother has friends. You could try the big house in Buidhe ... Robert Tenford's staff are mostly from the mainland, but he usually has an idea about what's happening around.'

'Tenford?' Carrick raised an eyebrow. 'I thought he was dead, sir.'

'This one is a nephew. He's running the business now.' Shannon swirled the remaining liquid in his glass and was thoughtful. 'You never met my own nephew, did you?'

'No, sir.'

'He's a good lad.' From Shannon, it was as near to praise as any human being was likely to receive. 'I wouldn't like to think ...' He stopped short and cleared his throat self-consciously. 'Well, there's your orders. Head ashore as soon as you're ready. I'll have Clapper Bell organize anything that's necessary as far as the *Thrift's* concerned.'

'And you, sir?' asked Carrick, rising. 'The engineroom were wondering –'

'I know.' Shannon pursed his lips. 'But I'm taking *Marlin* out inside the hour. We'll use what daylight's left in another sweep between here and Black Reef.' He sighed. 'It would take the whole damned Protection squadron a month to check every beach and every island around here, but we'll do what we can.'

* * *

34

Webb Carrick crammed a few items of kit into a duffel-bag, scribbled a note to Clapper Bell, then handed both to the duty steward to be passed to the bo'sun. He shoved an extra pack of cigarettes into the pocket of his uniform jacket, left his cabin, and made his way down the gang-plank.

He was walking along the pier and had passed beyond *Marlin's* bow when another figure scrambled up into view farther ahead, coming from a small dinghy tied against a rough wooden ladder. It was the girl from the catamaran. She saw him, gave a friendly nod, and waited until he reached her.

'When we saw you this morning and signalled we didn't know about the *Thrift*,' she said. Her voice held a faint huskiness and the dark grey eyes made no attempt to hide their curiosity. 'If we'd heard, well, we'd have tried to help.'

'You handle that boat of yours pretty well,' he told her. 'We were watching.' But even so, he mused, he hadn't seen enough. She was smaller than he'd thought, little more than up to his shoulder and probably in her mid-twenties. A supple, firm-breasted delight of a girl with a face and figure shaped close to perfection. He wondered what she'd look like in another outfit than that shapeless sailing jacket and those tight-legged sun-bleached denim jeans she wore with such tiny, featherweight moccasins. Yet the effect was still good, seemed almost natural with such a fresh, open-air complexion, that short yet softly curled dark hair. And he'd been right about her mouth, at any rate. It was generous, full, and with more than a hint of a slightly mocking smile as she accepted his inspection.

'Johnny said someone had glasses on us.' For a moment she let the amusement in her spill over. 'What do you think of the *Gooshgash*?'

'I like her lines – and how she travels.'

'She'll out-sail most in her class,' said the girl proudly. 'But what about the *Thrift*? What happened to her?'

35

Carrick played for safety. 'We're still trying to find out. She was lying derelict near Black Reef.'

'And the crew?' She read the answer in his silence and the grey eyes clouded for a moment. 'I met them a couple of times.' She seemed about to ask more, then to decide against it. 'Going up to the village? I am.'

They began walking along the pier. 'Decided to moor at Kenbeg overnight?' asked Carrick.

'I live here.' She looked at him strangely for a moment. 'I thought you'd know . . . from my father, I mean.'

An unwelcome suspicion edged into Carrick's mind. 'Your father?'

'There he is, on ahead.' A touch of amusement entered her voice. 'You've met, haven't you? I saw him leaving *Marlin*.'

Carrick looked along the pier and suppressed a groan. Sawny MacKenna stood at the pier entrance beside a pile of rusting fuel drums, watching them with a definite interest.

'We've met,' he agreed.

'I'm Aline MacKenna,' said the dark-haired girl with a twinkle. 'Has that father of mine been quarrelling with Captain Shannon again? I know he's pretty worked up about the *Mora* vanishing – not that I blame him.'

'They disagreed a little,' admitted Carrick as he saw the fisherman cross to meet them. But MacKenna seemed in a happier mood.

'You keep the strangest company, lass,' he declared with a mock sorrowful shake of his head. 'This one's name is Carrick, and he's from that instrument of persecution they call a Protection cruiser.'

'Nobody's perfect,' she told him. Then, ignoring Carrick for the moment, she asked, 'No word yet, Father?'

'About the *Mora*? Nothing.' There was what might have been a flicker of warning in the glance which passed from father to daughter. 'But there's still most of the lobster fleet out looking. And I've explained about Drammy

36

MacPherson to Captain Shannon.' It was innocently done, almost too innocently.

Aline MacKenna merely nodded. 'We searched up to Hammond Point, but there's nothing in that direction. After that, Johnny had to turn back – we've got to see Bob Tenford.'

'I'd remembered.' MacKenna's mouth tightened a little. 'Going home first, lass?'

'No – not now I've seen you. Johnny's waiting.' She turned to Carrick. 'I hope ... well, maybe there'll still be good news about these men who were on the *Thrift*.'

'There's always a chance,' said Carrick, knowing just how much the odds were against it.

They said goodbye and the girl walked briskly back along the pier towards her dinghy.

'A nice lass, even though I'm saying it about my own,' mused MacKenna. 'And a bad thing all this happening, especially now.' Something in his manner gave the words a particularly personal meaning.

'Bad ... for her?' asked Carrick. Along the pier, the dark-haired girl had reached the dinghy. She got aboard, untied the mooring rope, then, with a last wave towards her father, began rowing.

'Aye, she gets married next month,' said MacKenna softly. 'Her lad owns that queer catamaran thing out in the bay. Page is his name, John Page. He's a vet on the mainland, and wi' a bit of cash behind him into the bargain.' Abruptly he changed the subject. 'That carpet-faced skipper of yours will be leaving some men behind when he sails, am I right?'

'Four of us. We'll be working on the *Thrift*.'

'Just so – it's a polite way of putting it, anyway.' MacKenna stuck his hands in his pockets and considered for a moment. 'Well, there's a favour I'm going to ask. Come home with me for a minute, Mr Carrick. I want to show you something – and maybe once you've seen and listened you'll understand things around Kenbeg a bit better. Will you do it?'

Carrick nodded. He had a feeling it would do no harm to tag along.

They set off together. Beyond the pier, a single well-worn strip of tarmac wound for a short distance between the first few whitewashed cottages and their storesheds. Then it ended, to be replaced by a potholed track loosely surfaced with beach shingle.

'Not much sense in having anything better,' said MacKenna, at the same time exchanging a grave nod of greeting with a stoutly built woman who went past. 'There's just the one lorry on the island, along with an old jeep and a few bicycles. The sea's our roadway.'

'How many boats work out of here?'

'Ten now, though there used to be more. Too many of the young folk are going to the cities.'

Carrick had heard the same sad tale many times before. Each year that passed the whole Hebridean chain of islands felt the growing drain of depopulation. Empty cottages, abandoned crofts, rotting boats, closing school-houses showed the magnetic pull of the mainland's bright lights and big money.

'Who runs the drifter lying out there?' he asked.

'Tenford, the bulb man over in Buidhe.' MacKenna's voice showed little liking for the fact. 'Properly it should-n't be there – he's got a couple or so smaller boats he keeps on his own property. But he says there's no decent moor-ing for the big one.'

'He's a friend of your daughter's?'

'Tenford?' The fisherman shrugged. 'Young Page knows him, that's all.'

'I'd have thought having a project like that next door would help people in Kenbeg –'

'It does and it doesn't.' MacKenna stayed wooden-faced. 'We go up here now.'

38

They turned off the pebbled path and along a smaller track to where another cottage, slightly larger than the others, sat close under the shelter of a rocky outcrop. Even so, the thick stone walls and the small windows told their own story of the gale fury which could batter from the Atlantic in winter.

The cottage door was painted bright red. It opened as their feet crunched up the track – and Carrick's mouth fell open as he saw the girl standing watching them approach. She wore a bronze-brown skirt of lightweight tweed, topped by a shirt-styled white blouse and a bronze-brown wool cardigan, but what mattered was the rest.

The same face, the same figure, the same short dark hair and grey eyes, even the same slightly guarded smile of welcome was there.

'My other daughter, Arran,' said Sawny MacKenna proudly.

'Twins?'

'Identical twins. I married late by some folks' reckoning. But not too late.' MacKenna's pride was manifest. 'Their mother is dead these past five years, yet there's not a better kept house in Kenbeg.'

At the cottage door MacKenna made the introductions. Arran MacKenna's voice was like an echo of her sister's as she ushered them in.

'Of course, this father of ours wouldn't say anything when you met Aline – he never does.' She gave a sigh, part despairing, part affectionate. 'It's his own little surprise for strangers.'

'And why not?' demanded MacKenna. 'What's wrong with showing the two prettiest daughters a man ever had?' He beamed at Carrick. 'In you go, now.'

Arran MacKenna led the way into the front room. Carrick laid his hat on the table then glanced appreciatively around. It was a big room, surprisingly large when he remembered the cottage's outside appearance. The furniture was in old, dark, well-polished wood and a peat fire smouldering in the hearth completed the traditional picture. But a multi-band transceiver set was on a shelf beside one window, the curtains were in gay, modern fabric and there was electric lighting where he'd expected to find old-style oil lamps.

'The Electricity Board ran a power cable out to the islands about eighteen months ago,' said the girl, anticipating his question. 'They probably wouldn't have done it if they hadn't been given the chance of a big central heating contract for the greenhouses over on Buidhe – still, we got the benefit.' She glanced at her father. 'Mrs Bain from the village told me there's still no word about the *Mora* – but that the fishery cruiser brought in the bank boat. What happened to it?'

'They found it off Black Reef,' said MacKenna shortly. 'The rest can wait.'

'I see.' But she was far from satisfied. 'And you're not in trouble?'

'No – if there's trouble it's for someone else,' rumbled MacKenna. 'That's why I brought the Chief Officer home. Come through the back, man. What I want you to see is out there.'

They left the girl and went along the cottage's narrow hallway. There was a plain wooden door at the far end and MacKenna opened it, waving him into the low-roofed storeroom beyond. Lobster creels lined one wall, an old net hung draped from the rafters, and the rest was a jumble of boat stores, from engine parts to cork floats.

'Over here.' MacKenna stooped beside a bench and dragged a white enamel bucket from under it. Water slopped over the rim as the bucket grated over the stone floor. 'See for yourself,' he invited.

There were about a score of oysters lying one on another in the bottom of the bucket. From their size they were a mixture of both young and mature, but their shells gaped open and the flesh within was black and dead.

40

'That's what I mean by trouble.' MacKenna scooped out one of the shellfish and tossed it on the bench. 'The whole damned lot were poisoned – and plenty others the same, left dead or dying.'

Carrick picked it up and frowned as he sniffed the decaying flesh. 'Where'd you find them?'

'Find them?' MacKenna gave a bitter shake of his head. 'There's no finding involved. I've been working up a hatch of my own – nothing big, just a wee experiment to see if there was sense in it. I used a tidal pool in a cove to the north, built a water-sluice and dredged up stock. There were near to four hundred oysters in that pool, Carrick. Then four days ago I found them like this – and now they're not worth collecting for shell-grit.'

Easing the shell wider, Carrick examined it with greater care. Oyster farming was an idea more than a few people were nibbling at along the Hebridean coast. Overfished, the big, fat Hebridean oyster had come close to dying out in its natural state. Re-establishing the native stock in artificial areas or importing fresh oyster spat from places as far apart as Norway and Portugal, the successful could find a steady, high-priced demand from the food markets. For the unsuccessful – well, these things happened.

But MacKenna stood waiting, the man's silence conveying indignation better than any words.

'Oysters can die for plenty of reasons – most of them natural.' Carrick laid the opened shell back on the bench. 'Who says these were poisoned?'

'Aline's lad, John Page.' MacKenna knocked the dead oyster off the bench, sending it splashing back into the bucket. 'He saw them and he made the tests. It was rat poison that was used, rat poison with a cyanide base.'

'If you've a report like that from a qualified vet why didn't you pass it on to us?'

'Why?' MacKenna snorted. 'Because whoever did it didn't leave his name an' address behind. So what good would it do? What good came of the reports we made

41

about the lobster troubles – the stolen pots, the cut ropes, all the rest that's been plaguing us?' His face hardened. 'But that doesn't mean we don't know who to blame. It's the mainland boats every time.'

Carrick stifled a sigh at the inevitable. The mainland boats were big seventy-foot open-sea vessels, each laying two hundred or more lobster creels where a little island boat might lay thirty. The mainlanders came to lay, to harvest until they were full, then headed home again without ever touching land. When conditions were right, the occasional foreign boat nipped in too – laying its float-marked trail one night, lifting it the next. And generations of islanders had hated both with an impartial fury.

'Where have the mainlanders been working?'

'To the north – but where they're seen by day and where they're skulking after dark are different things.' MacKenna shrugged. 'Well, I've told you, whatever good it does.'

'It would help more if you'd tell me something else,' mused Carrick. 'And I'm not thinking of oysters, MacKenna. I'm more interested in other things.'

'Like where I was last night?' MacKenna sucked his teeth in thoughtful style. Carrick watched his face, seeing the expression smooth its way into more benevolent lines. 'Well, at least you're more civil about it than Shannon,' admitted the fisherman. 'And – all right, why not? For the last couple of nights I've been sitting out at the oyster cove wi' a shotgun over my knees, hoping the man who used that rat poison would come back wi' more.'

It was smoothly done, briskly told – and Carrick didn't believe a word of it, no matter how the shellfish had died. But he nodded his thanks, and MacKenna seemed satisfied.

'Now that's over I've a wee job to do here,' he said, waving vaguely around the storeroom. 'And you'll be busy yourself. So –'

'I can find my own way out,' said Carrick. 'And if you remember anything else – well, you know where I'll be.'

42

He left the storeroom, closed the door behind him, and walked back along the little hallway.

'Finished?' Arran MacKenna stepped out from the living room in a quick movement which showed she must have been waiting for his return.

'Uh-huh.' He gave a twitch of a grin as the cool grey eyes met and held his own. 'He was telling me about the oysters.' How a domineering old blackguard like MacKenna could have had one daughter, let alone two, so magnetically attractive was a minor mystery on its own.

'John showed Aline and me the test results,' she volunteered. 'It was some kind of cyanide preparation.'

'I'll take your word for it,' he told her gravely. 'And your father's too, of course.'

Arran MacKenna flushed, but took one of the cigarettes he offered. Carrick lit it and then his own. 'Right now, though, I've another call to make. Where do I find Drammy MacPherson's mother?'

'That's simple enough.' She leaned back against the doorway, thawing a little, yet still on her guard. 'It isn't far, just a walk round the bay and beyond the point where the south channel begins. Keep to the beach, and you'll see an old fishing boat lying on the shingle above high-water mark.' She read the lift of his eyebrows and nodded. 'That's where they both live. And – well, don't rush her if it comes to questions. Jean MacPherson doesn't think as clearly as other people.'

'I'll remember,' promised Carrick, feeling no particular urge to leave.

'Anything else?'

'Well –' He rubbed his chin. 'To be honest, I was wondering how to tell you and your sister apart.'

She laughed. 'There's a way. Why?'

'Just interest – personal interest. Aline seems pretty useful on a boat. How about you?'

'The same.' Arran MacKenna rose to it as if challenged.

'We can work a lobster boat between us as well as any two men on the islands.'

'That's something I'd like to see,' mused Carrick. 'Only you haven't got a boat – not until they find the *Mora*.'

She shrugged. 'Aline's going to try to borrow one from Bob Tenford over on Buidhe. If that doesn't work, we'll maybe borrow Johnny's catamaran. Either way, there are twenty creels lying out near Dearg Island, and they've got to be lifted. We'll be going out in the morning.'

'Could your father borrow one of the other Kenbeg boats?'

She shook her head. 'He could – but these are our creels, Aline's and mine. Whatever we make from them we keep.'

'What time are you going out?'

'About eight –' Arran MacKenna stopped and frowned. 'Now look, I didn't mean –'

'But I did. Mind if I come?'

Her lips shaped a faint pout, as if tasting the possibility. Then she nodded. 'Why not? People around here would like seeing a Fishery man trying his hand at some decent work.'

From the cottage he took a direct-line route across the hummocked grass slope towards the south channel's point. Halfway there, a single siren-blast made him glance back towards the harbour pier. *Marlin* was leaving. A gathering froth of water showed at her stern as she edged out from the wooden piles, her bow swung slowly seaward, and then, in a way so familiar he could almost hear the ring of her telegraph, she suddenly began to pull ahead. Her wake thickened and widened, catching the little boats in the bay and sending them bobbing at their moorings.

Very soon the fishery cruiser passed where he stood, heading down-channel, the throb of her exhaust echoing across the water. He walked on, while *Marlin* widened the gap until at last her stern had disappeared from view beyond the point and the water between Kenbeg and Buidhe was once again placid and empty.

Another five minutes took him to his destination. The old fishing boat Arran had described lay ahead, forlornly stranded where grass met shingle some thirty feet above the tangle of seaweed which marked the tide's limit. Some long-forgotten wave in a giant storm might have tossed the boat to where it rested, but now, its hull edged by tall weeds and thick brambles, it was a land-rooted derelict of flaked paint, bared wood, and rusted metalwork. Wheelhouse and mast had vanished, a rough door was set midway along the frail hull, and a length of stovepipe protruded at an angle from the deck, smoke scattering gently from its peak.

Carrick eased the cap back on his head and gave a mild whistle of surprise. Wrecked, abandoned boats were no major curiosity among the islands – come to that, most Hebridean villages had the unlovely habit of using their beaches as a dumping ground for garbage. But he'd never come across anything quite like this one before.

The door in the hull swung open when he was still a good hundred yards distant, and he slowed his pace as two men came out into the open. They looked back as if saying goodbye and then, as it shut again, began walking towards him.

'Looking for Mrs MacPherson?' asked the first to reach him. 'I'm John Page – Aline told me she'd met you.' The owner of the crimson catamaran was tall and raw-boned with close-cropped fair hair and a nose which showed all the signs of having once been broken. He held out his hand and his grip was surprisingly gentle. 'You're Carrick, right?' He turned to his companion. 'Bob, this is the Fisheries character Aline talked about.'

'Robert Tenford from Buidhe,' said the second man. The bulb-grower had a plump, tired-eyed face with a slight double chin and thinning, prematurely grey hair. Heavier in build than Page, he was at the same time the smaller by a couple of inches. Carrick placed them both in their mid-thirties. 'We'd an idea you'd show up here.'

Carrick nodded. 'She's about the only link we've got with what happened to the *Mora*.'

'Of course.' Something which could have been a nervous flicker showed in Page's expression. 'Bob and I came over to make sure the woman was all right – Aline's idea. Jean MacPherson prefers outsiders to the locals, but even then she doesn't encourage visitors.'

'Neither did her son,' grunted Tenford.

'Did?' queried Carrick. 'You think that's how it is?'

Tenford shrugged. 'I don't know any more than anyone else. What interests me more personally is what happened to the *Thrift*.' He stuck his hands in his jacket pockets. 'Is it true the safe was blown open?'

'It was still in one piece when we brought her in,' said Carrick mildly.

'Good. When do the police arrive?'

'Tomorrow sometime.' Carrick saw no reason to conceal the fact. And of the two men, despite his gruffness, Tenford seemed the friendlier.

'Then I hope they bring someone from the bank,' declared Tenford. 'Friday's the end of the month. I've got men looking for wages – and the money for it is in that safe.'

'Carrick . . .' John Page gnawed his lip. 'What about the crew of the *Thrift*? Surely you've some idea what happened to them?'

'If he had, he wouldn't tell us,' said Tenford pointedly. 'Am I right?'

Carrick shrugged. 'So far, there's nothing to tell.'

'Exactly.' Tenford turned to go. 'Anyway, we've told Jean MacPherson she's to let us know if she needs help. And come across to Buidhe for a drink if you get the chance – I like visitors. Just remember to use the south landing stage. It's nearest the house.'

John Page hung back for a moment. Then, with a nod, he set off after his friend. Once they'd gone, Carrick continued towards the derelict boat, seeing for himself the damage which had made her worthless. From her bow on, almost eight feet of the keel had been smashed away below the waterline, leaving a gaping space now half-choked with weeds. Once, incongruously, she'd been the *Silver Queen* – the name still clung in obstinate paint-streaks to her bow, a barely visible trace of someone's long-passed pride.

Carrick crunched across the shingle to the makeshift door, knocked, waited, and knocked again. He heard a slow shuffle of movement from inside, then glimpsed a face peer out from one of the small, brass-rimmed port-holes. The face vanished, there was another shuffle of movement, and at last the door creaked open.

'Well?' The woman who stood in the doorway was middle-aged, drab and unkempt, with no sign of hope in her face. 'Is there news?'

'No.' He shook his head. 'But Captain Shannon thought I should have a talk with you.'

'A talk . . .' Her voice died away. Jean MacPherson was still in middle age, but she moved with the slow weariness of an old, sick woman. She wore a stained woollen dress which hung like a sack, her feet were in battered, down-at-heel brogues, and her grey, straight hair framed a face cast in habitual bitterness.

'Can I come in?'

'Aye.' She turned and shuffled back inside. Carrick followed her, stooping to avoid the beam of the low doorway.

Inside the boat, the atmosphere was stale and smoky. Whatever her past pride, the *Silver Queen* was now a shell of mainly bare ribs and warped planking. From the deck above, the chimney-pipe he'd noticed ran down to a rusted cooking stove where a fire glowed a dull red. A rough wooden partition sealed off the smashed bow, a pair of dirty, crumpled army blankets hung from a rope to act as a curtain towards the stern, and most of the few scraps of furniture in sight looked as if they'd been salvaged from the original wreck.

'I'll make a cup of tea.' She lifted a blackened kettle from beside the stove and thumped it on the cooking plate. 'Sit down – what's your name anyway?'

'Carrick. I'm Chief Officer on *Marlin*.' He settled himself on one of the two stools by the stove. A man's oilskins hung on a wooden peg against one bulkhead, a few shelves had been fitted at another point and beneath them, on an old locker, sat the only thing of value in sight – an old-fashioned silver picture frame holding a faded photograph of a family group.

'There now –' Jean MacPherson clattered two heavy mugs on a small table beside the stove, then added a bag of sugar and opened a tin of milk. She followed his gaze, and for the first time her face seemed to lighten. 'Aye, it's bonny, isn't it?' She crossed over and brought it to him. 'We had that taken on Archie's eighth birthday. Went all the way to Oban to a proper photographer.'

Gently, Carrick took it from her. The print showed a man, a woman, and a small boy in a stiffly formal pose. The man was young and broad-shouldered, dressed in Sunday-best suit and stiff white collar. The woman by his side was stout but gay in a floral-patterned cotton frock, while the schoolboy between them, the most solemn of the three, had his hair brushed down and wore kilt, sporran, and all the other adornments of juvenile Highland dress.

'Very nice.' He handed it back. She stood where she was, the photograph cradled in her arms. As far as Jean MacPherson was concerned, there was obviously more reality in that picture than in her surroundings, more belief in a schoolboy named Archie than a missing man called 'Drammy' MacPherson.

'How old is your son now?' asked Carrick quietly.

'Archie?' She had to drag herself back to the present and think. 'He was nine when it happened. Fifteen years – aye, twenty-six he is now.'

'What happened to your husband?'

'The sea.' She clutched the photograph tighter. 'This was his boat.'

'It happened here?' He stared at her, shaken. 'But –'

'He called her the *Silver Queen*. She worked the great lines.' Pride was back in the voice, shining in the words. The men who worked the great lines, those tricky mile-long strands of viciously barbed Kirby hooks, were still the aristocrats of the fishing industry.

Then, just as suddenly, the light died. She shuffled back, replaced the picture, and sat down heavily on the stool opposite.

'Why haven't you found my Archie?'

'We're looking,' he assured her. 'So are the Kenbeg boats. Everyone's doing what they can.'

'Are they?' She shook her head. 'The Kenbeg boats are looking for the *Mora*, not for my Archie. It's Sawny MacKenna's boat, that's what matters to them.'

'But MacKenna's friendly with your son, isn't he?'

'Friendly?' She broke off, muttering to herself for a moment. 'There's friendship and there's fear. There's fear and there's debt. I know what's being thought – that Archie stole the *Mora*, and then had something to do with what's happened to the bank boat.'

'Who told you that?'

She shook her head. 'Do people always have to speak before you know?'

Carrick sighed. 'Mrs MacPherson, all I know is there's a man and a boat missing from this island. You admit that your son was drinking pretty heavily that night?'

'He has his weaknesses.' She pursed her lips. 'I know the name they give him.'

'He didn't tell you where he was going or what he was doing?'

49

She shook her head.

Carrick tried another tack. 'If he'd taken the *Mora*, he'd have had to sail down the channel, past here. Did you see the boat leave?'

She nodded. 'I saw a boat – it could have been the *Mora*. I don't know for sure.'

He gnawed his lip, wondering. 'What about last night, Mrs MacPherson? Did you see any boats leave the harbour?'

'I did. That yacht thing –'

'The catamaran?' Carrick sucked in a breath. 'When?'

'The first time would be about ten o'clock.'

'The first . . . you mean it came back?'

'It did.' She gained a grey satisfaction from his interest. 'It came creeping in here again about four in the morning, not a light to be seen on her. And it was out again within the half hour.'

'You're sure?'

'With my son missing and me watching that channel for every boat that comes?' The kettle began steaming, but she ignored it.

He frowned. 'You had two visitors just before I came. One of them was Page, the man who owns the yacht. Did you tell him what you'd seen?'

She gave a sudden, bitter laugh. 'Tell him? I told him nothing. How do I know if my Archie is alive or dead – or why?'

'I see.' Carrick looked at her, knowing how little weight her evidence might carry yet somehow believing her. 'Could I see your son's things?'

'He's not here to object.' She shrugged. 'He sleeps through at the stern.'

He thanked her, rose, and pushed through the blanket screen. The stern section was roughly divided into two cabins. One was the woman's. The second – his mouth tightened as he saw Drammy MacPherson's quarters. An old mattress on a camp bed frame, some bedding, and a scattering of empty bottles were its main fitments. A locker in one corner held a few items of clothing. He lifted the mattress and let it drop again, and then his eyes strayed back to the locker. There was an inch or so of space between its top and the roofline above.

Carrick stood on tip-toe, reached up, and felt around in the gap. His fingers brushed something soft and compact, and he pulled it out – a small oblong package wrapped in oilskin. He listened, heard no sound from the woman, and unwrapped his find.

What was inside posed its own surprise. Drammy MacPherson, an island drunk, who lived in a stranded hulk, had almost a hundred pounds in cash and a bank book with five times that amount to his credit. The bank book had been issued by the inter-island branch of the Bank of Central Scotland – by the *Thrift* lying out there in the bay.

Carrick quickly re-wrapped the parcel and put it back in the hiding place. Then he went back to the woman.

'That's all I need for now,' he told her.

She didn't look up. The kettle was bubbling on the hob, but the promised tea seemed forgotten.

Quietly, gently, he stepped past the woman towards the door.

Chapter Three

Dusk was near by the time Carrick made his way along the beach to the spot where his shore party had set up camp. Two pup tents sat side by side, a bottled gas stove burning in front of them, its flame hissing round the base of a bubbling pot.

The tide was going out – and a hundred yards off shore the grounded *Thrift* was beginning to show more of her hull above water. Their collapsible boat was tied to her stern, and he could see two figures moving inside her cockpit.

'Hello, sir!' Able Seaman Marshall, a bantam-sized Liverpool man, bobbed out of the nearest pup tent. 'P.O. Bell's gone out to see how she's lyin'. He said he wouldn't be long.'

Carrick nodded. The immediate concern now was a delicate balance of mooring lines and a judgement of how the bank boat's keel was settling. One mistake could heel her over on her side and complicate the entire job of refloating. 'What's in the pot?'

'Bo'sun's special – stew.' The seaman grimaced. 'Says it's his own recipe.'

'Sounds ominous.' Carrick chuckled. He glanced at the tents. One was filled with a miscellany of equipment and some piled bedrolls, the other housed a portable R.T. set and a couple of folding stools. 'Who's our fourth man?'

'Spencer, sir.' Able Seaman Spencer was one of *Marlin's* youngest hands, a dour Lowland Scot.

'Fine. Had any visitors so far?'

'Not formal like,' said the seaman, shaking his head. 'We saw a couple o' fishing boats – they came in pretty close an' took an interest. And there were two characters givin' us a good look-over from farther up the beach.'

'One tall and fair, the other smaller, grey-haired?'

'That's 'em, sir. They headed in for the village after a spell.'

John Page and his friend Tenford – well, mused Carrick, he'd have been surprised if they hadn't shown some degree of curiosity. But if Jean MacPherson's story was worth anything, Page had some questions to answer. And one might be how the money in Drammy MacPherson's bank account had been earned.

A hail from the *Thrift* came thinly across the water and showed he'd been sighted. Clapper Bell and young Spencer emerged from the cockpit, dropped down into the rubber boat alongside, and began paddling for the shore. There was a forty-horsepower outboard engine mounted on the collapsible's stern, but for the short distance involved it was superfluous. In little more than a minute the lightweight nosed against the beach and Clapper Bell leaped out, splashing through the shallows towards them while his companion secured the craft with a tripod grapnel.

'How does it look out there?' asked Carrick.

'No' bad, no' bad at all, sir.' Clapper Bell lifted the pot's lid, sniffed and nodded. 'She's doing nicely.'

'The stew or the *Thrift*?' queried Carrick patiently.

Bell grinned. 'Both. The second mate made things easy for us when he grounded that boat – I reckon she'll sit smooth as a baby. We've time to eat first, if you feel like it.'

'All right.' He waited while Bell sent the two seamen searching for plates. 'Clapper, you were with Captain Shannon when he had his last tangle with Sawny MacKenna. What about this Drammy MacPherson? Was he involved?'

53

Bell scratched his head. 'No. MacKenna was on his own then – it happened up at the Monach Isles, to the north. We caught him shooting seals without a licence.'

'Tell me about it.'

'It's simple enough. We heard the shooting an' saw his boat close inshore through the bridge glasses – he'd half a dozen carcases aboard, worth twenty quid a pelt. But there was mist around, an' the moment he saw us he steered that damned *Mora* of his into it. Took her on through a rip-tide channel where the rocks were sharp enough to slice bread, dumped the seals, an' had fished a box of cod aboard by the time we managed to get to him the long way round.' Clapper Bell shook his head at the memory. '"Seals?" says he. "Now I'd some grey blankets spread out for dryin', Captain. Must have been them you saw. Signals? Och, I saw a flag or two and heard some shouts. But it was misty – for all I knew it might have been some-one's birthday." So help me, that's what he said.'

'And he got away with it?'

'Ended up demandin' an apology from the Old Man!' The audacity of the idea had left a considerable impression on *Marlin's* bo'sun.

They ate the stew, heavily flavoured, slightly burned but otherwise edible. There was plenty of coffee to wash it down, and afterwards Carrick postponed moving for long enough to smoke a cigarette. Around them, the sun was setting in a final glory of red and gold against black which only sea and rock produce. As he watched, a trio of lob-ster boats came up-channel in line astern, their engines a soft, slow gargle above the wash of the sea.

At last, reluctantly, he rose to his feet and signalled the others. Marshall and Spencer took the weight of the portable pump unit between them, carried it down to the rubber boat, and loaded it aboard. A moment's effort refloated the boat, then they boarded it and began pad-dling towards the *Thrift*.

A sharp, shrill whistle sounded at the same moment as the boat began moving – a whistle from somewhere not far out in the bay. While the blast still echoed, a short figure in a green rubber scuba suit came scrambling out of the bank boat's for'ard hatchway. Carrick swore angrily as the diver went over into the water, bobbed chest-deep for a moment, then sun-fished down out of sight.

'Over there, sir –' Spencer, in the bow, pointed farther out. Carrick glimpsed a dark shape in the dusk-greyed water and then it vanished.

'Engine!'

Clapper Bell yanked hard on the starter, and the outboard howled to life. Throttle jammed open, the rubber boat began foaming forward, her crew straining for the trace of an aqualung's bubble trail. Once again it was Spencer who spotted the tell-tales rising, some forty feet beyond the *Thrift* and heading out into the bay. Still in less than ten feet of water, the scuba diver became a vague, almost ghostly outline below the surface as they first overtook and then slowed alongside the bubbles. Foot-fins kicking, the diver kept desperately on.

'Marshall, let's have that grapnel – and quickly!' Carrick leaned over the side while the seaman reached for the treble-hooked iron and its attached line. This fish, at any rate, wouldn't get away.

But next moment the odds changed in sudden, nerve-shattering style. The metallic whang of a spear-gun came simultaneously with a harsh thud as two feet of barbed steel shaft hit the rubber boat's starboard air cylinder and stayed embedded, its tip protruding on the far side. A steady hiss told of pressurized air leaking free – the scuba diver's comrade had taken a new, determined hand.

'Hold on!' Sheer instinct prompted Clapper Bell as he rammed the throttle wide open and threw their bow round to present a narrower target. But in a matter of seconds they had other problems. The thick rubber of the starboard cylinder was rapidly losing its shape – and the scuba diver they'd come within an ace of collecting had vanished from sight.

'Turn back to the *Thrift*,' decided Carrick bitterly. 'And keep down, all of you – one of those spear-bolts could do the same thing to your head.'

They crouched low, tensed for the next spear-gun whang. But it didn't come, and they reached the bank boat with air still sighing from the punctured, flattening cylinder. In itself, that was no disaster – just a simple rubber patch repair job. What mattered was why the scuba diver had been snooping. Carrick left his men to drag boat and contents aboard the *Thrift* and made a quick check. The mooring lines hadn't been touched. Hard aground, her hull now a good three feet exposed, the bank boat was like a full cup of water standing in a shallow tray. For the time being, at any rate, she seemed safe enough. He looked seaward for a moment, gnawing his lip, then turned round.

'Let's get that pump set up,' he said wearily. 'There's work to do.'

It took an hour and a half, part of it by torchlight, for the little auxiliary pump to finish the job of emptying the *Thrift*. By then, the tide was fully out and the keel rested in mere inches of water. While the pump was still sucking, Carrick took a torch and prowled alone through the wet chill of the main saloon. Feet squelching over the sodden carpet, he played the torchbeam around seeing here and there a dark brown strand of devilweed or a gasping, flopping dab-fish left marooned and helpless.

The safe, at least, was still intact. Carrick tried its handle, then crossed over and squeezed his way behind the tiny, toy-like counter. A purple-domed jelly-fish throbbed gently, stranded half-in, half-out of an opened desk drawer. He peered at the lock, and his mouth set in a moment of tight-lipped anger. It had been forced, the wood splintered, the drawer emptied.

'Sir –' Clapper Bell had padded down into the saloon and at the same time Carrick realized that the pump had stilled. 'We're finished. I've put Marshall and Spencer on makin' a better job of blockin' that engine pipe.' He laid one large hand on the safe, then slowly lifted it again. 'I just thought o' something. This tin box here –'

'Well?'

'It's pretty big.' Bell sucked his teeth reflectively. 'Aye, big enough to hold a body. It wouldn't surprise me.'

The thought wasn't completely new to Carrick. He nodded. 'We'll find out once tomorrow comes, Clapper. But from now on we'll keep a double watch aboard. I'll take first stint with Marshall, then you take over with Spencer.'

Bell grunted. 'I'll tell them. Need any help down here?'

Carrick shook his head. 'I'm prowling, nothing more.'

The crew quarters aft came next on his list. Three tiny cabins, each with a bunk, a locker, a mirror and a wash-basin – the *Thrift's* crew lived simply when on duty, yet in its own way each cabin conjured up a soft-grained image of its user.

In the first, where water still dripped steadily from the bedding, he guessed the occupant from the locker's contents. A rough homespun tweed jacket, a hand trawling line and a pair of greasy, worn overalls added up to Henderson, the coxswain engineer. In the middle cabin, a huddle of adventure-story magazines, a leather-cased transistor radio and an impressive array of shoes probably meant young Andrew Sword, Shannon's nephew. That left Wilson, the manager, for cabin number three – and only a bank manager would have favoured such a sober line of conservative grey ties and stiff white collars. His reading taste was equally sober. The small bookshelf held some assorted reference books, a two-volume work titled *The Botanists' Encyclopaedia*, and a few paperback editions of the classics.

He swung the torch in a last arc around the manager's cabin then eased the beam down towards the cabin floor as something small and metallic glinted in the light.

Slowly, almost reluctantly, he bent down and picked up the cartridge case. He knew the type – it came from a .38 automatic. Once again he used the torch, patterning its beam in deliberate fashion around the cabin walls.

It didn't take long. A small, round hole had been punched in the wood panel lining a bulkhead behind the manager's bunk – a hole just on the level of a man's chest. The bullet which had caused it had sunk only a fraction of an inch below the surface, as if it had already encountered resistance before it had hit the panel.

Carrick had seen enough. The *Thrift* should refloat at high tide, and all that would be needed as that happened was a gradual slackening of her mooring cables to allow for her regained buoyancy. But now, when he radioed *Marlin*, he'd have plenty to add to his message.

It was the kind of report which would bring no comfort to Captain Shannon – and in his own mind, Webb Carrick gave up any last hope for the missing men's chances. The cartridge case resting cold and damp in his hand, plus the bullet in the wall, tipped the scales against the chance they were alive. Then the new raid on the *Thrift*, the drawer he'd found forced open and empty ... the two scuba divers had taken a desperate risk. Why?

He gave a wry shrug and dropped the brass cylinder into his pocket. Captain Shannon might have towed the *Thrift* to the Rathbeg Isles on a mere wild, stubborn hunch. But whatever had happened aboard the bank boat, the three islands were firming as part of its background – while the boat itself had taken on the character of a smouldering fuse. When the explosion came, Carrick wondered just how far the blast would reach.

Leaving the narrow cabin, he climbed up on deck. The moon was rising, a fisherman's moon, full and yellow, framed by fat, lazy clouds.

'Bo'sun!' He waited until Clapper Bell joined him from the bow. 'I'm going ashore to radio *Marlin*. We'll stand the watches as arranged until the next tide. If we're lucky, we'll have her moved before dawn – and afterwards, I'm going lobstering.'

'Eh?' A momentary frown slid across Clapper Bell's face, then gave way to a crinkling, incredulous grin. 'You mean wi' one of old MacKenna's girls?'

'With both of them.'

'Well . . .' Petty Officer Bell spoke in solemn, deliberate style. 'I'd remember one thing. Women an' lobsters have somethin' in common. Damn sharp claws . . . sir.'

At 8 a.m., the day fine and dry, the wind little more than a fresh breeze from the south-west, Webb Carrick walked on to the wooden pier at Kenbeg village. He'd been up since five, and across the bay the *Thrift* now floated on an easy, even keel. They'd eased her out of the shallows on the peak of the tide.

Breakfasted, shaved, only a little short of sleep, he saw that plenty of other people had had an early start. Most of the lobster boats had already left the harbour and the only two remaining had their engines fussing and men aboard.

'Good morning.' A gruff voice boomed briskly, and he turned, surprised. Robert Tenford sat on a nest of fish boxes behind the pier shed, a pipe between his teeth, his arms folded. 'The girls didn't think you'd show up, Carrick.'

'You mean they've gone?'

Tenford removed the pipe briefly from his mouth and used it as a pointer. 'No, they're still getting ready. They're using the catamaran – my spare boat has engine trouble, and I'm already using the drifter.'

Carrick followed the pipestem's wave. The crimson catamaran lay about a hundred yards out, but Tenford's big drifter had been shifted to a berth alongside the pier. Men were moving aboard it, and the hatches were open.

'Fishing?' he queried.

'Me?' Tenford found the idea amusing. 'Not enough money in it, and too much hard work. No, they'll take her across to Buidhe and load a cargo of daffodil bulbs for the mainland. On the trip back they'll bring in bone-meal and some other stuff. That's what I got her for, to cut down on shipping costs.'

Carrick looked across the bay towards the smaller island with its long rows of greenhouses and regimented planting beds, and nodded. 'It makes sense. MacKenna told me you'd a problem when it came to mooring over there.'

'Small boats are easy enough, but something that size –' Tenford gave a heavy-shouldered shrug. 'She's safer here.' He sucked hard on the pipe. 'Sawny MacKenna's had some bad luck lately – and losing the *Mora's* only part of it. He told you about the oyster farm?'

Carrick nodded. 'Cyanide poisoning, according to him.'

'That's what John Page found and John knows his stuff.' Tenford eyed him for a moment. 'Well, if what I think's right and Drammy MacPherson took the *Mora* out while he was three parts drunk, then MacKenna may have lost a boat – but he's also seen the end of a lot of trouble.'

'You mean from MacPherson?' Carrick showed his interest. 'What makes you think MacPherson could be behind the poisoning?'

'The poisoning – and maybe a lot more,' growled Tenford. 'Look, you talked to Jean MacPherson yesterday. She was friendly enough, right?'

'Within reason,' he agreed. 'Though she did say something about MacKenna which didn't make sense –'

'About a debt.' Tenford took it for granted. 'MacKenna and her husband were crewing the old *Silver Queen* the night it was wrecked. The story goes that if they'd tried to ride the storm in the open they'd have been safe enough. But MacKenna lost his nerve and made MacPherson try to bring her in.' He took the pipe from his mouth and spat expertly between the wooden slats of the pier. 'Anyway, MacKenna was washed ashore, half-dead and rambling about how it was his fault – then a week later they found MacPherson's body.'

'So MacKenna tried to befriend the son!' Carrick nodded in understanding. 'But Jean MacPherson didn't forgive so easily –'

'Forgive?' Tenford gave a dry, humourless laugh. 'You saw how she lives, what she's like mentally. As for her son – well, MacKenna may have tried hard to make things up. But the way Drammy hit the bottle, the way he must have lived on a steady diet of what MacKenna did to his father . . . it makes sense to me.' He looked past Carrick and, his expression changing, rose to his feet. 'Leave it at that for now.'

Her dark hair covered by a bright bandana worn turban-style, the MacKenna twin coming towards them was dressed ready for work. The rest of her costume was a heavy-knit red sweater and old whipcord slacks tucked into calf-length rubber boots. She stopped, a basket swinging in one hand, and inspected Carrick in whimsical fashion. 'All ready to go, Mr Carrick?'

He grinned and guessed. 'Ready and waiting, Arran.'

'Aline,' she corrected.

Tenford gave a snort of amusement. 'If you're like me, Carrick, it gets wearing on the nerves.'

Aline MacKenna took it in reasonable humour. 'For everybody. Even my John makes the odd embarrassing mistake.' She handed Carrick the basket. 'Well, you can carry this, for a start – it's bait. Arran's out on the cat with John, getting ready.'

'We've been pretty busy ourselves,' murmured Carrick.

'We noticed.' She put her head questioningly to one side. 'Any trouble getting her refloated?'

'I was going to ask that myself,' said Tenford, shifting his weight from one foot to the other. 'Well, Carrick, what's the latest about it all?'

'Nothing much more than we knew already – that some-one tried to sink her.' The cartridge case in his pocket and the spear-gun episode were things he'd decided to keep quiet about until *Marlin* returned.

'Then that part, anyway, was more than just gossip!' Tenford pursed his lips. 'Well, I suppose banks are insured against most things. But what about the human factor – Wilson the manager and the other two who were aboard?'

Carrick shook his head. 'We don't know.'

'That's bad enough on its own,' said Aline MacKenna, frowning. 'But this idea that Drammy MacPherson might be involved is ... is just ludicrous. He wouldn't harm a fly.'

Tenford shrugged. 'That's so much wild gossip, and island gossip is more poisonous than most. Unless – Any comment, Carrick?'

'I prefer dealing in facts – though they're in short supply right now.' He hefted the basket and glanced at the girl. 'You were away from home while all this was happening, weren't you?'

She nodded. 'Yes. I was on the mainland, trousseau shopping in Edinburgh. I got the morning plane back to Barra yesterday, and John brought me up to Kenbeg on the *Gooshgash*. He told me about Father's boat as soon as we met.' A look of caution crossed her face. 'Why – does it matter?'

'Just curiosity,' he assured her. 'You sounded very sure about MacPherson.'

'I am,' she said confidently. 'And it's time we got started. What about you, Bob? Are you going across with the drifter?'

Tenford shook his head. 'No. Doctor Perris is due in this morning and I said I'd meet him.'

'Here again?' She blinked. 'I thought he was in Kenbeg while I was away.'

'He sailed in three days ago,' agreed Tenford. 'But he's keeping an eye on some youngster in the village – a

62

possible appendix case. I want him to take a look at one of my gardeners who's gone on the sick list.'

'Doctor Perris is our nearest G.P.,' she explained for Carrick's benefit. 'He's usually here only once a fortnight, unless there's an emergency.' She thought for a moment. 'I'd heard the Roberts baby was ill – she must be the one. Well, anyway, we'll need to go now.'

They said goodbye and left Tenford smoking his pipe, hands deep in his pockets.

'Quite a little empire he's got,' mused Carrick as they walked along the pier and past the bustle aboard the drifter. 'How many men does he have working for him?'

'Bob Tenford?' She considered briefly. 'Twenty or so – but we don't see much of them. They've got their own quarters on Buidhe, and only two or three of them are Kenbeg men. Bob says fishermen don't make good gardeners.'

The catamaran's dinghy was tied near to the pierhead. Carrick climbed down first, stowed the basket aboard, then helped Aline down. But she shook her head as he went to handle the oars.

'I'll do that.'

He didn't argue, but untied the mooring line, then settled back in the stern. She slid out the oars, brought the dinghy's head round, then pulled away with a short, steady stroke. Her hands were small but strong. There was no ring on her left hand, but he noticed a faint line of white across the ring finger showing that her engagement ring had only been removed because of the work ahead.

There was no sign of life aboard the *Gooshgash* until they bumped alongside. Then, as the girl scrambled aboard, her sister's head popped out of the cockpit. Arran MacKenna was in a similar rig but, unlike her twin, her head was bare.

'You found him!' She seemed pleased at the fact, and shouted down into the catamaran's cabin. 'John, they're here –'

A muffled reply echoed up and she translated. 'We're all set to go. Webb, if you hitch the dinghy to the stern and then cast us off from the buoy, we'll get moving.'

He obeyed. As the catamaran's cable slipped free and he began coiling it on the low pulpit deck, the *Gooshgash's* outboard began throbbing. By the time he'd made his way back to the cockpit, the crimson yacht was already creeping down the channel.

'Hello again.' John Page greeted him with a nod. The young vet was at the controls, one hand resting on the steering wheel, the other resting fingertip-style on the throttle lever. A yachting cap was crammed over his stubble of fair hair, he wore a pair of old blue overalls, and his manner seemed more relaxed than when they'd last met. 'There's coffee on the stove – the girls can show you around.'

Carrick thanked him and squeezed down the narrow companionway into the cabin below.

'Over here,' invited Arran. She was standing by the tiny compact galley, where the daylight streamed brightly through a porthole to gleam on her hair and play shadow tricks around her mouth. The catamaran's frame swayed with gentle life as it met the channel's deepening swell, and she balanced lightly against the motion. 'Aline's tidying the other cabin.' She laughed. 'According to her, John keeps this boat like a pigsty.'

He looked around while she poured coffee from a metal pot into a heavy china mug. The interior layout was a minor revelation in space-saving. On the one side of the cabin was the galley, complete with a two-burner cooker, sink, and grocery cupboard. Next to it was a big main-berth settee. A folding centre table sat between the pillars of the upper deck supports, and on its other side was a second settee, a toilet compartment, and more cupboard accommodation, including a glass-fronted bookcase-cum-cocktail cabinet. Black leather and light natural mahogany made a striking yet practical colour scheme. Up towards the twin bows, beyond a small, half-opened door, he caught a glimpse of Aline MacKenna in the for'ard cabin, where another berth sat crossways across the width of the catamaran.

'Two berths here, three up front,' said Arran. 'The two you can't see are pretty small. They run inside the hull floats, and you practically need a shoe-horn to get in or out. Like it?'

'That's an understatement,' said Carrick, frankly fascinated by every detail down to the way in which a chronometer and a repeater compass had been set into one of the main deck-beams above his head. He took a mug of coffee from her, sipped it, and gave a rueful shake of his head. 'But my kind of pay cheque wouldn't run to this style of layout.'

'You couldn't manage it on lobsters either,' mused the girl. 'And John's a pretty nice character into the bargain.' She poured another mug of coffee for herself, put down the pot, and looked at him carefully. 'I'm still wondering why you came along.'

'Meaning?' He sat on one of the cool black leather settees and tossed his cap with its gold-braided Fishery Protection badge on to a handy shelf. 'Something worrying you?'

'The *Thrift* in the bay, these missing men, Drammy – and yet you're here.' Her mouth closed tight for a moment. 'Why?'

'Because there's not much else I can do right now, and I happened to want to come.'

'I see.' She was far from satisfied. 'Nothing to do with my father?'

'Should there be?' He sat back, enjoying her nearness yet sensing the tension developing between them. She didn't answer for a moment and then, as her sister came out from the other cabin, he grabbed the chance to switch the conversation back on safer lines. 'All fixed back there, Aline?'

Aline wrinkled her nose. 'As near as can be. But once we're married, John's going to need some training.'

'Most of them do,' said Arran with a forced brightness. 'Like some coffee?'

'No – I'll go and see if I can help.' She moved past them and up the companionway to the cockpit.

Arran waited until she had gone, then took a deep breath. 'Well . . . ever worked a lobster line before?'

'Never, but I don't mind learning.' He took out his cigarettes and gave her one, then a light, their hands barely brushing in the process.

'Thanks.' She took a long draw on the tobacco and leaned back against the centre pillar. 'There's not much to it. All you've got to remember is that their claws aren't for ornament.'

'I knew a fellow down in Ayrshire once,' mused Carrick. 'He used to go lobstering in an aqualung outfit. Anybody around here ever tried it?' He raised an innocent, questioning eyebrow.

'Skin-diving?' She shrugged. 'No, but it might be an idea.'

'It might.' He was thinking of the scuba diver he'd seen the night before, small in build – small enough, in fact, to have been a girl. And another diver farther out, a diver who could handle a spear-gun. The MacKenna girls might, between them, constitute a resolute force if they had a particular aim in view. He pushed a grin on his face. 'Well, one thing's sure – I've found how to tell you two apart.'

Her face thawed to a slight smile. 'Tell me.'

'Aline has a mole, very small, just under her left cheekbone. You haven't. I only noticed it when you were together just now.'

'There's that,' she agreed. 'Then there's something else.' She sat down beside him and held out her left hand, palm upmost. A broad white line puckered down the skin from forefinger to wrist. 'I did that when I was a kid – sliding down a rope while we were gull's-nesting on the cliffs.'

He took the hand and inspected it gravely. 'Must have been pretty painful.'

'Not half as painful as the leathering I got for doing it.' She smiled again, more openly. Then, as the grey eyes grew darkly serious, 'Webb, why did you come?'

'Because I wanted to.' He still held her hand. But his other arm slipped round her waist and she made no resistance as he pulled her closer. 'Let's leave it at that.'

'But –'

He stopped her with his kiss. For a moment, her lips stayed passive, then suddenly they were alive and demanding against his own.

'Well?' he asked eventually.

'It's an answer,' she agreed soberly. 'But – it's still not the only one, is it?'

They went up to the cockpit in a little while, when the yacht's gradually increasing roll told them they'd left the channel behind and were in open water. The catamaran's outboard still throbbed and her mast was bare of sail.

'No sense in it,' said John Page gloomily. 'This is going to be bus-run stuff. Still, it's better than yesterday morning, I suppose. I caught the tail of that storm when I was going down to collect Aline, and it was no easy trip.'

'I'm not sorry I missed that one.' Carrick grinned. He rubbed his chin self-consciously as he saw Aline MacKenna eyeing her sister and then himself with a peculiar interest, and quickly concentrated on where they were.

The *Gooshgash* was heading up the west coast of Kenbeg with the low, rocky shape of Dearg Island growing nearer to port.

'Far to go?' he asked.

'No.' It was Arran who answered. 'We've got the creels laid in about fifteen fathoms off Dearg, on this side. There's plenty of rock on the bottom.'

Lobsters liked rock – and with the island there to act as a natural breakwater against the main Atlantic, conditions should be close to ideal, guessed Carrick. The depth was right too – most of the big West Highland lobsters lived between the ten- and thirty-fathom mark.

'*Homarus vulgaris* – that's what we called them at vet college,' said Page, easing the wheel a fraction. 'The ones the girls get around here are pretty good, well over your minimum, Carrick. You won't need a tape measure.'

Carrick draped himself back against the cockpit rail and grinned at the thrust. Any lobster caught which measured less than nine inches from tip of beak to end of tail had to be put back, that was the regulation. But there was little need to enforce it. The market was for the bigger fellows, and the Hebridean brand of crustacean was more likely to be close on double that length.

'Sawny MacKenna was telling me how you helped him over that business of cyanide poisoning,' he said cheerfully. 'Where's your regular practice? On the mainland?'

'Uh-huh.' Page kept his attention ahead. 'After a fashion, anyway. My folks run a hotel near Applecross – strictly a tourist trap. I base around there.' His mouth twisted into a self-conscious grimace. 'It's quiet, but it's enough.'

'For all this?' Carrick looked around the cockpit, frankly disbelieving. He knew the Applecross stretch – a vast, sea-edged uprise of mountains with an occasional crofter's cottage and a thin dusting of sheep, outnumbered ten to one by wild deer.

'He used to have another practice, a big one,' said Aline MacKenna sharply. She pursed her lips. 'But leave it to John and you'd get the idea he was the original playboy of the Western Isles.' She ignored Page's frown. 'What he doesn't bother to say is that he worked himself into a hospital bed two years back. His health still won't stand a full-time job.'

'According to my mother it won't stand marriage either,' reminded Page gently. 'But I don't wave that around like a flag.'

She flushed and fell silent. Page gnawed his lip, glanced at her for a moment, and then Arran saved the situation.

'There it is – first marker's coming up.' She pointed ahead, and started them moving. 'Webb, fetch up that basket of bait. John, you know what to do?'

'You'll use the dinghy and I'll take you alongside them,' acknowledged their helmsman patiently. 'Though why you can't do it from here –'

'Because it's easier and because you might get the boat's paint scraped and create hell about it. Right, Aline?'

The other twin nodded and, as her eyes met Page's, showed a dying edge of indignation. 'At least if it was a boat he'd talk about it.'

The catamaran slowed, her bow wave dying to a chuckle as she turned into the current and crept the last few yards towards the first bobbing marker. It was a round slab of cork, painted white. Carrick pulled the dinghy up alongside the yacht and followed the MacKenna twins aboard. Then, still secured to the *Gooshgash* by the long painter rope, they drifted down to the marker.

'Get it in and start hauling,' ordered Arran.

He set to work, bringing in coil after coil of the cold, wet cordage while Page used an occasional touch of the yacht's throttle to hold them steady. At last, the oblong shape of the creel began to shimmer up from the grey-blue water.

'Well?' Aline drummed her fingers impatiently on the gunwale. 'Anything?'

'Lucky first time.' He heaved in the last yard of cord and swung the creel aboard in a spatter of spray. Inside the cage of net, big pincer claws waving a slow, searching protest, a heavy pink-blue lobster sat angry and waiting. 'What now?'

'This.' Arran leaned forward, her short dark hair ruffled by the breeze, and opened a flap of the creel. She reached in, gripped the lobster's barnacle-speckled shell from the rear, and dragged it out into the open. 'Aline –'

Her sister was ready. As the left claw groped in snapping anger she slipped a thick elastic band over the pincers, holding them closed. The other claw snapped – and was summarily treated in the same way.

'Two pounds if it's an ounce.' Arran laid the angry, helpless captive in the bottom of the dinghy. Carrick rebaited the creel with a gutted herring from the basket and they lowered it down to the sea bed again, then released the float. The catamaran's engine growled louder and the dinghy bounced in its slow wake as they headed the fifty-yard distance to the next marker.

The second creel was empty. The third held a captive, but one that the Fishery rules said had to be set free. Under its abdomen lay a mass of small, round, red globules – it was a female carrying spawn. Carrick felt a moment of amusement as it sank back down. He was under no illusion about what might normally have happened. A few strokes with a brush would have left the female clean for sale.

They moved on, with varied fortune. They got two lobsters between the next three creels, but the fourth came up with a massive two-foot-long specimen in prime wrath.

'Easy now.' Arran reached inside the creel and heaved the monster into the open. 'Eight pounds, maybe more.' She looked at him, a sudden devilment dancing in those grey eyes. 'Your turn, Webb. And hurry up. It's heavy.'

'Me?' Carrick stared in dismay at the waving, clacking pincers then at the two rubber bands thrust into his hand. Cautiously, warily, he timed his move and secured the nearest claw. But the other set of pincers swung and snapped down on his fingers. He gave an unrestrained yell of pain.

'Stay still!' The two girls made it an order.

'All right – but get the ruddy thing off,' he demanded.

70

'Don't pull,' pleaded Aline. 'You'll pull its claw off at the joint. Just wait.'

For a fraction of a second the pincers eased as the lobster moved for a better grip. Carrick jerked his hand free, the jaws snapping shut a hairsbreadth later.

'If you'd pulled the claw from it we'd have lost money,' said Arran with minimum sympathy. Her sister already had a band over the waving pincers, and she dumped the monster down.

'Nobody wants a one-claw lobster.'

'What about a one-handed sailor?' complained Carrick. But they ignored him.

Nine more pots yielded only four more lobsters. Then they found an unexpected gap in the line of markers.

'Rope must have frayed.' Arran frowned. 'We'll need to take a line from the other markers and drag for it.'

'If I'd an aqualung I could find the thing in a couple of minutes flat,' said Carrick, still nursing his fingers and mentally cursing all things with claws and temperament.

'Well, we haven't, and creels cost money,' said Aline impatiently. 'But we'll do it in a little more comfort.'

They worked themselves back to the catamaran, climbed aboard, and John Page quickly produced a grapnel and a spare length of nylon line. Aline went below to warm the coffee pot, leaving her sister to work the line over the side. Arran handled it expertly, letting the cord run out between her fingers until she felt the grapnel touch bottom, then raising it a double hand-span to avoid rock snags.

'John . . .'

Page nodded and slid the throttle lever forward. Slowly, the engine's beat rising to little more than a throaty whisper, they began dragging. Twice they covered the distance of the gap, then a third time, the line still held lightly between Arran's fingers. Suddenly it jerked, she shouted, and Page reacted in an instant, killing the engine while more of the line streamed out and disappeared into the water.

71

The *Gooshgash* drifted to a standstill, Arran already pulling on the line while her sister hurriedly joined her from the cabin. Then Arran stopped and frowned. 'There's something wrong.'

'Snagged a rock?' asked Carrick, taking the thin nylon rope from her hands.

She shook her head. 'No, it's moving. It . . . it's just too heavy.'

He tried for himself, felt the line quiver, and knew she was right. Whatever was down there was free of the sea bed. He hauled slowly, muscles straining, peering into the water while the wet line gathered at his feet. Then, at last he saw a vague, blurred shape rising at the end of the line.

'Page –'

The young vet looked and nodded, his mouth closed in a tight line. Carrick turned to the dark-haired sisters and knew from their faces that they'd also seen what was down there.

'We'll have to bring him aboard. It may not be pleasant.'

They nodded but said nothing, and he began hauling again. Slowly, steadily, the loose-limbed body on the end of the grapnel rose towards them and finally broke surface.

Close beneath it, hanging like some grotesque pendant, was the missing lobster creel.

'Take it in over the stern,' said Page hoarsely. 'I'll give you a hand.'

Between them, they dragged the body and its burden aboard. The dead man was young and hadn't been in the water for long. He was dressed in worn blue overalls and a heavy wool shirt, but one seaboot and sock were missing. His face was marked by minor cuts and gashes and the long black hair was laced with silt and bottom weed.

'You know him?' asked Carrick quietly.

'We all know him,' Page told him soberly. 'It's Drammy MacPherson.' He touched the lobster creel with his foot. 'This could explain a lot.'

Carrick moved the fisherman's body a fraction, seeing how part of the creel's broken rope had wound round the man's left leg while his right arm was entangled in the stout mesh of the covering net. 'You mean he was raiding the lobster line?'

'It's happened before, and if he was drunk –' Page shrugged. 'Look, we know he'd been hitting the bottle before he took that boat out. If he was careless enough to get that rope round his leg, and the boat lurched . . .'

'If.' Carrick closed his mouth hard on the word.

'What else?' Page scowled his bewilderment. 'I'm a vet, not a doctor, but I know a drowned man when I see one. And there's a simple reason for these abrasions –'

'Caused by bottom rock, I know.' Carrick rose slowly to his feet. 'A man goes out stealing lobsters and he's drunk – all right. But there's no lobster in that creel, Page. It couldn't have got out on its own, and why shove your hand inside an empty pot – unless you're so blind drunk you couldn't take a boat out of Kenbeg in the first place.'

'Then . . .' Arran MacKenna moistened her lips. 'Then what else, Webb?'

He looked at her for a long moment, saying nothing. Fresh in his mind was Robert Tenford's theory that the dead man at his feet had been behind MacKenna's troubles – that, and the memory of the bank books hidden in the old, wrecked *Silver Queen* on Kenbeg shore, a hulk which formed a link with that other past.

'Page, if you've got a spare piece of sailcloth –'

'I'll get one from the locker.' Page nodded, understanding. 'We can put him for'ard, on the pulpit deck.'

'And the creel with him, just as it is,' added Carrick grimly. If the doctor due at Kenbeg had arrived on the island then he would be the man to decide what might have happened. But for the moment Carrick was taking no chances.

73

Five minutes later the crimson catamaran was throbbing its way back towards Kenbeg Bay. She breasted through the waves, her mainsail drawing extra speed from the breeze. Drammy MacPherson, island drunk and now a waterlogged corpse wrapped in an old nylon studsail, was making his last trip home in dark, impressive style.

Chapter Four

Marlin was back. Carrick saw her grey silhouette alongside the pier as the catamaran came up-channel and swung into Kenbeg Bay. Surprised, he glanced at his watch. It was barely 11 a.m. – which meant, whatever the reason, that she'd arrived at least two hours ahead of schedule.

Another new arrival was tied up next to the fishery cruiser, an arrival which brought a murmur of relief from John Page. The vet took one hand off the brass-rimmed wheel and pointed ahead. 'There's Doctor Perris' boat, Carrick – the one with the black hull. Well, that's a help, anyway. I'll tell the girls.' He leaned over and shouted down to the cabin. 'Aline, Perris is still here!'

'Which should be a weight off Mr Carrick's mind,' her voice echoed back, the chill behind the words plain. The MacKenna twins had gone below several minutes earlier, sharing a look which showed they wanted to talk alone, undisturbed.

Page gave him a wry, almost sympathetic grimace. 'You'll find Doctor Perris is all right – knows his stuff, too. He's been around this part of the world for a good few years now. Sails that boat of his single-handed and prefers it that way.'

Carrick nodded, watching with a fresh interest as they grew nearer. The doctor's boat was a broad-beamed, forty-foot cabin launch with a high, old-fashioned superstructure but immaculate paintwork.

'Calls that boat of his the *Emma-Dee*,' volunteered Page, making an effort to keep the conversation going. 'You know, stretching out M.D. into a name – he's got a liking for that sort of thing.'

'He's welcome.' Carrick grunted. He could see a few faces watching them from *Marlin's* deck. Well, if anybody thought he'd been on a pleasure trip they'd soon know better. There would be the matter of explaining to Captain Shannon exactly why he'd been out at the lobster line in the first instance – but even that small, fiery Superintendent of Fisheries would accept that it had been worth while.

Arran and Aline appeared in the cockpit again just as the catamaran's outboard throttled back ready for her swing in alongside the pier. They stood silent, avoiding looking at each other. Whatever they'd discussed, no agreement seemed to have been reached. Still without a word being said, Aline moved forward to the *Gooshgash's* bow line leaving Arran to cope with the stern. Carrick took his cue from them. As the catamaran crept in, he stepped lithely across the narrow gap between the boat and one of the pier ladders, climbed up, caught the mooring lines they threw him, and secured the yacht fore and aft to a pair of empty bollards.

As he finished, he heard heavy feet hurrying towards him.

'The Old Man's lookin' for you, sir.' Clapper Bell gave a perfunctory, unhappy salute. 'They arrived in about an hour ago, an' – well, maybe you'd better no' keep him waitin' too long, the mood he's in.'

'Right.' Carrick could imagine what the bo'sun really meant. 'Tell him I'm coming straight over, Clapper. But get a couple of men and a stretcher across here while you're at it.'

'A stretcher . . .' Clapper Bell looked down, saw the sailcloth bundle at the catamaran's bow, and gave a sniff of immediate interest. 'Like that, eh? Who is it?'

'MacPherson, our missing fisherman. Any idea where this Doctor Perris has gone?'

Bell scratched his stubble of hair. 'I saw him in the village earlier on, before *Marlin* arrived, an' there's nobody on his boat now – I know that much. Well, I'll get the stretcher organized an'' – one eyelid lowered in a brief, conspiratorial wink – 'an' I'll let the Old Man know why.'

'Thanks.' Carrick gave a flicker of a grin, thinking of Captain Shannon's blood-pressure. He let the bo'sun start on his way, then turned to the pier's edge and waved the others up from the catamaran. The girls came first, John Page following them in reluctant fashion.

'I was thinking of staying with the boat –'

'No need,' Carrick assured him. 'We'll keep an eye on things until the doctor arrives.'

'Well . . .' Page gnawed his lower lip, undecided.

'There's one thing we could do,' reminded Arran unhappily. 'Somebody has to tell Mrs MacPherson.'

'Somebody – but not from the village,' said her sister shortly.

Arran smoothed her dark, ruffled hair and nodded. 'I know, but John could – he's an outsider, but she knows him.'

Page showed his dislike of the idea, but sighed agreement. 'I might as well do it now and get it over with. Want to come along, Carrick?'

'Sorry. I'm on my way to see Captain Shannon.'

'Shannon – and the police you've been waiting on?'

'If they're aboard, yes.' Carrick thumbed towards the catamaran's bow and its silent cargo. 'They'll want a full statement from all of you about this before they're done.'

'I'll come with you, John,' decided Aline MacKenna. 'I'll hang back a bit, but I'll be there if you need me.' She turned to her sister. 'Arran?'

'No. I'll look for Dad – let him hear about Drammy at first hand. That's better than having him pick it up on the

77

village grapevine.' As Page and her sister set off, she hung back for a moment. 'Webb –'

'Yes?'

She looked along the pier. Aline and Page were walking slowly, arm in arm. 'You're right, Webb. There is something you should know, something that matters. We were talking about it in the cabin, on the way back.'

'Going to tell me?'

She shook her head. 'Not yet. It's – well, it's up to my father. But believe me, whatever you may think, he knew nothing about what happened to Drammy and he didn't rob the bank boat.'

'But it might not look that way?' Carrick rubbed his chin. 'Tell him something from me, Arran. Tell him this is no situation to fool around with. There are still three men missing, probably already dead for all we know. The longer he holds out, the more trouble he's getting himself into.'

'I know. But – well, it isn't easy for him, either.' She took a step closer to him, her grey eyes warm and somehow pleading for understanding. 'Webb, whatever happens –'

'Let's leave it until it does.'

She nodded, touched his arm lightly, then had gone, hurrying after her sister. Carrick watched her for a moment, then headed for the fishery cruiser.

A seaman was waiting for him at the top of the gangway as he came aboard.

'Captain Shannon?' queried Carrick.

The man nodded. 'Straight off, sir. He's in the wardroom.'

Carrick went below, into the warm, diesel-fragranced atmosphere of the ship, the low background whine of her generators familiar music to his ears. A growing murmur of voices as he neared the wardroom flat warned him what to expect as he entered the long, narrow cabin.

Three strangers in civilian clothes were grouped with Shannon round a table which was partly covered by an unrolled chart. Their conversation ended abruptly, the visitors staring at him with undisguised interest.

'So you're back, mister.' Shannon waved a vague, general introduction. 'This is my Chief Officer, gentlemen – the man we've been waiting on. Carrick, this is Chief Inspector Dawe and Sergeant Wylie, county police.' The two policemen, Dawe tall and thin, his sergeant a younger man and broadly built, greeted him with a nod. 'And this is Mr Campbell, Henry Campbell, from the Bank of Central Scotland.'

'Head office, inspectorate division,' said Campbell in a thin, determined voice. He was a small man with a pale, mouselike face and a neat, ginger moustache. 'Captain Shannon has just finished telling us you've found this missing fisherman.'

'Like to fill in the details, Carrick?' asked Chief Inspector Dawe. 'That's why we got the map out. In fact, you might as well start with what happened earlier. It'll save time in the long run.'

He told them, and they heard the story out in silence. Captain Shannon gave a loud sniff as he finished.

'Just one thing, Carrick. This trip out to the lobster ground – what was your reason for going?' He gave a suspicious frown. 'I expected you to be here when I got back.'

'From all accounts the MacKenna twins are a good-looking pair,' mused Chief Inspector Dawe, with a cold humour. 'Well, there's always good sense in encouraging a moderate amount of local contact.' He turned to Carrick. 'I'd like that cartridge case you found.'

Carrick nodded and handed it over. 'The bullet is still in the cabin panelling.'

Dawe nodded. 'We've seen it. We've already been aboard her with Mr Campbell.'

'Sir?' Carrick glanced questioningly towards Shannon.

The Superintendent of Fisheries chewed his lip and nodded. 'Campbell opened the safe. The money's still there, still intact – nearly all of it, anyway.'

Campbell cleared his throat, embarrassed at being put in the limelight. 'At a rough check, there's about twelve hundred pounds missing out of the fifty thousand – but that could have been used for normal business at places of call before ... ah ... before this happened. Exactly what business I can't tell yet. The drawer you found forced open last night would normally contain the office daybook and routine cash sheets. Now they've gone, it'll be difficult to reconstruct the voyage record.'

'Which is probably why they were taken.' Chief Inspector Dawe lowered himself into a chair and lit a cigarette. 'Somebody had an afterthought.'

'As for the crew, I've brought their personal files.' Campbell coughed delicately. 'All excellent character ratings, of course. Peter Henderson, the – ah – seaman has been five years on our staff, always given satisfaction. John Wilson, the manager, is a widower and he's been with the bank all his working life – a most responsible individual. Young Andrew Sword ... well, your nephew showed considerable promise, Captain.'

'What matters to me is he's twenty years old and my sister's only child,' said Shannon grimly. 'What's been done about contacting relatives?'

'Well ...' Campbell bit his lip. 'So far all they've been told, all anyone has been told, is that the *Thrift* was badly damaged in Tuesday night's storm and that a search is going on for the crew. That's on police instruction, of course.'

'For everybody's sake, mine included.' Dawe grunted. 'What else can we tell them at this stage? Anyway, it keeps the press off our backs.' He frowned. 'Now what? Finding the money still in the boat doesn't make much sense. The notes were new, consecutively numbered – maybe that scared off whoever organized this. But even so, given the

80

right contacts there's plenty of ways of doing a deal in hot money. One third the value is the usual trading rate.'

'Presuming they had the keys to open the safe,' murmured Carrick.

Dawe shrugged. 'Right now just about everything's guesswork, Chief Officer. I'd have thought any half-intelligent crook would have been ready and equipped to deal with that kind of problem. Maybe they were, maybe something happened to scare them off. I don't know.'

'Does it have to add up to robbery?'

'We've talked about other reasons,' admitted Dawe with a quick glance towards Shannon. 'But what kind of reason makes any real sense? Short of imagining someone going berserk with a gun I can't think of any.' He shook his head. 'Ach, maybe all this wouldn't have happened if the *Thrift* had been fitted with something approaching a decent security system.'

'We considered all adequate precautions were taken.' Campbell was frigidly indignant at the criticism. 'She has an alarm bell system installed. She has an explosive-proof safe with vibration-operated safety bolts.' He sniffed. 'And I'd remind you that my bank was one of the founders of the inter-bank reward fund. We offer a constant reward of a thousand pounds to anyone who helps identify or convict a bank robber.'

'Big deal,' muttered Sergeant Wylie, who'd been peering out a porthole. He flushed at the sudden silence he created. 'What I mean is –'

He was saved by a knock at the wardroom door. Jumbo Wills stuck his head into the cabin.

'Well?' demanded Shannon.

'We've more or less located Doctor Perris, sir,' reported the second mate. 'He was seen crossing over to Buidhe Island.'

'Tenford was hoping to get hold of him,' said Carrick, nodding agreement. 'Like me to go and fetch him back, sir?'

Captain Shannon dismissed the second mate with a nod, then considered for a moment. 'Yes. There's something else you could do at the same time. It's this business of the MacPherson woman saying she saw MacKenna sneaking in and out of the bay in that catamaran. It would help if someone not quite so – so emotionally involved could confirm her story. Someone on Buidhe, for instance.'

'I'll ask Tenford,' agreed Carrick. 'But he may not like it. He knows the MacKenna girls, and John Page is a friend.'

'Friendships can wither when the heat's on,' said Chief Inspector Dawe. He took a long pull on his cigarette, yawned softly, and shook his head. 'This sea air's hitting me – much more of it and I'll have to prop my eyelids open. But while you're fetching Doctor Perris we'll collect the bank book MacPherson was hiding. After that we'll run a check with some of the mainland lobster buyers to see if they knew him. This MacPherson business could be coincidence, but as things are – well, we've got to soak up every possibility that comes along.'

'Right.' Carrick was on his way to the door when a thought struck him. He looked back towards Shannon. 'What about the keepers at Black Reef, sir? Could they help?'

Shannon gave a slow, heavy shake of his head. 'That's one reason why we got here ahead of schedule. They spotted the *Thrift* drifting, and that's the beginning and end as far as they're concerned. Oban Radio's putting out a signal to all steamship traffic and coastguards in the area asking for details of any unusual sightings, but there's no dividend so far, mister.'

Carrick left them and went on deck. He stopped for a moment by the gangway, watching the stretcher party returning with their burden. The ratings clattered their way past him, but Clapper Bell, following close behind, stopped and raised a hopeful eyebrow.

'Everything okay, sir?'

'Aye.' The bo'sun leaned over the rail and spat down the gap between ship and quay. 'Well, here's someone comin' who could change that.'

Carrick looked along the pier and took a hurried step back from the rail. Sawny MacKenna was hurrying towards the fishery cruiser, his cut-down seaboots flapping round his ankles.

'Where's our pack-boat, Clapper?'

'Moored aft,' said Bell. 'Eh, what about MacKenna?'

'Tell Captain Shannon –' Carrick grinned maliciously – 'I've already left.'

The trip across to Buidhe was short but pleasant, the water a rippling blue-green, the wind light against his face. Beneath the boat the water was clear enough to show the white sand of the channel bed, broken by occasional clusters of listless, bushy weed or by the inevitable debris of any bay – a shattered, half-buried oil drum, glinting bottles, once a snake-like length of abandoned, rusted wire cable. Ahead, a small army of gulls sat along the little island's rocky shore and refused to be disturbed by his coming.

He turned the pack-boat in towards the south landing stage. It was a mere projection of planks running from an outcrop of shore on spindle-legged supports, a dinghy and a small speedboat already moored alongside. As he cut the engine and drifted in the last few feet a man strolled into view from the shore end and stood watching him, hands on hips.

'Lookin' for someone, friend?'

'Doctor Perris,' said Carrick briefly. 'He's over here, isn't he?'

'Unless he's swimmin' back.' The man, middle-aged, truculent-jawed, dressed in a khaki shirt and slacks topped by a heavy, grease-stained wind-cheater, took the pack-boat's line and tied it round a projection. 'You're from the fishery cruiser, right?'

Carrick nodded and stepped on to the walkway. 'How do I get to the house?'

'Suppose I check that he's there first – save you some trouble.' The man slouched ahead of him to the shore. A few feet back, a low hut was concealed behind some bushes. 'Hold on an' I'll find out.' He went inside, closing the hut door behind him. Through the small, grimy window Carrick saw him lift a telephone, wait, then have a brief conversation with whoever was at the other end, glancing out a couple of times as he spoke. Then the telephone went down and the man came out, a new friendliness in his manner.

'The house it is, friend. I'll show you the way.'

'I can manage.'

The man grinned, showing tobacco-stained teeth. 'I'm headin' that way, anyway. No trouble.'

'Official escort?' queried Carrick.

'Me?' The man shook his head. 'I'm the mechanic around here – Farley's the name. I came down to do a job on the speedboat engine, that's all. I need some extra tools, an' I was going back for 'em when I saw you.'

From the hut, they followed a path bounded by a series of well-tilled plots of fine dark soil patterned by neat heaps of rotting seaweed, destined to be dug in as compost. Farther on, they reached the first of a series of greenhouses, each filled with tier upon tier of growing plants. A few workers moved around them, busy on a variety of tasks. It was a peaceful, prosperous scene – Buidhe's riches were being carefully tended.

At last, rounding a clump of young trees planted to form a natural windbreak, they reached Tenford's house. Buidhe's owner lived in a compact two-storey block, flat-roofed, modern in structure and design. Behind it lay a scatter of small out-buildings, most of them crude cinder-block structures.

'Staff quarters?' queried Carrick.

His escort grunted. 'Not these, friend. They're store-houses – our livin' huts are farther up, near the north end. Makes it easier to keep an eye on anyone tryin' to sneak over from Kenbeg at low tide.'

'You don't like visitors?'

The man frowned. 'It's a private island, an' Mr Tenford wants it kept that way.'

Their approach had been noticed. Robert Tenford stepped into view on the porch of the house a moment later, waved his thanks to Carrick's escort, then waited, beaming. 'Nice to see you, Carrick – though I didn't expect it to be so soon. Farley's message said you wanted Doctor Perris. Somebody hurt?'

'No. . . . We found Drammy MacPherson's body,' said Carrick, mounting the steps to the porch. 'It was tangled up in the MacKenna lobster pots.'

'Well now!' Tenford pursed his lips. 'I tried to give you a hint something like that might have been going on.'

'I remember,' agreed Carrick. 'Anyway, we'd be happier if the doctor carried out something approaching a post-mortem.'

'That sort of thing would give me the shivers.' The bulb-grower rubbed one hand lightly across the knuckles of the other. 'Still, it's your business, not mine. Except – if you've found MacPherson then what about the *Mora*? She must have drifted on the rocks somewhere in the area.'

Carrick shrugged. 'It's possible. Where's Doctor Perris? Inside?'

'Eh?' Tenford blinked, then gave an apologetic nod. 'Yes – come on in. We were having a drink.' He led the way. Inside, the house was an expanse of natural wood panelling with sheepskin rugs scattered over the polished parquet floors. Tenford guided him to the right, into a long, broad lounge which ended in a full-width picture window looking straight out towards the south channel.

A table was set with bottles and glasses, and the man sitting in an armchair by the window rose at their approach.

'Henry, this is Chief Officer Carrick, from *Marlin*.'

Doctor Henry Perris, a short, square man with a round, bland face tanned until it might have been a moon cut from brown paper, gripped Carrick by the hand. He was an old man, with bushy white eyebrows and an almost completely bald head. But, though he might be in his seventies, his grip was strong and firm and he moved and spoke in a way which showed his years were no burden.

'If you're here as a patient I'm warning you this is my mid-day break,' he warned cheerfully. 'And I don't like my drinking time being broken.'

'He's found a body,' said Tenford, heading towards the table. 'What'll it be, Carrick? Whisky or –' he reached for the gin bottle – 'maybe you'd prefer some admiral's ruin?'

'Whisky, thanks –with water fifty-fifty.' Carrick watched Tenford pour, took the glass, and turned back to the doctor. 'The man was a local fisherman, missing for two days –'

'Drammy.' Doctor Perris nodded his understanding. 'I know him, and I'd heard he'd disappeared. In fact, I'd been thinking of looking in on his mother once I'd finished over here. With this happening, I'll need to – the woman's mental state is pretty threadbare at the best.'

'John Page has gone to tell her.' Carrick sipped his drink but refused Tenford's offer of a cigarette. They were in a heavy silver box, a box as expensively simple as everything else in the room.

'Somehow John always ends up drawing the dirty jobs,' mused Tenford. 'Henry, it seems Carrick wants you to examine the body. But – well, look, Carrick, how much of a rush is this? Doctor Perris isn't quite finished over here.'

'Anyway, I'd prefer to finish what I've started,' said the older man firmly. 'I'll put you in the picture, Carrick. One of the gardeners has been damned fool enough to cut himself pretty badly on an old tin can he dug up. There's no permanent damage, but I've given the fellow an anti-tetanus shot. That means a twenty-minute wait to make sure he doesn't react the wrong way.' He glanced at his watch. 'I'll need about another quarter-hour, including tidying up the dressing, before I'm ready. Suppose I come across to Kenbeg once that's done –'

'Or you could wait for him, Carrick,' suggested Tenford. 'Have another drink or, if you like, I'll show you around.'

'I'll settle for the guided tour,' Carrick told him. 'I saw enough on the way across to be interested.'

'Right.' Tenford drained his glass, then waited while Carrick did the same. 'Henry, you know your way around. Supposing we meet you down at the landing stage in twenty minutes or so?'

'I'll be there,' promised Doctor Perris. 'Just don't hide the bottle on your way out.' He was still chuckling as they left him.

Outside, Tenford stopped on the porch for a moment to set his pipe going. Match in hand, he peered into the bowl, then, when the glow was to his satisfaction, he asked, 'What do you know about the bulb market?'

'Nothing.' At the back of his mind, Carrick had a vague memory of himself as a small boy patiently watching a wizened bulb in a glass bowl. 'Except that there seems to be money in it.'

'Money – and risks.' Tenford steered him down from the porch and along a path edged with closely mown turf. 'My uncle started this place on bulbs alone, tulips, daffodils, the rest. They're still our financial backbone. But since I took over I've tried to develop from there.' He stopped outside the first of the greenhouses, opened the door, and gestured Carrick in.

As the door closed, the rise in temperature blanketed around them. From one end to the other, the greenhouse shelves ran in long sweeps of budding and blossoming exotics – orchids and cyclamen, cineraria and primula, then a riot of colourful begonias. The warm, moist air was heavy with their scent – and laced around them hung a web of piping and thermometers, humidity gauges and heating units.

'This unit stays at a steady sixty degrees,' said Tenford, fondling the leaves of the nearest plant, a delicately hued primula. 'Equivalent to a mild summer's day, with fully controlled humidity. There's money in this kind of flower and plant right through the winter months – provided you're organized and have a steady marketing pattern.'

'The overheads seem fairly high.' Down at the far end of the building, a tennis-court's length away, a gardener came into view. He saw them, touched his cap, then continued his routine, moving slowly, inspecting each boxed plant in turn. 'Staff problems, for instance – I've heard you don't use island labour.'

'Not more than I can help.' Tenford shrugged. 'I need skilled labour, and that nearly always means mainland men. They live in a bunkhouse, they work long hours, they find the Kenbeg people have no particular love for them. But they draw good money – so they stay.'

They left the greenhouse, crossed to its neighbour, and went in. This time the temperature seemed to soar, a dry heat which brought perspiration to Carrick's face. The plant boxes were smaller, filled with a coarse, sandy mixture and covered by an endless variety of tiny green, already fleshy sprouts.

'This is the dry house, for cacti.' Tenford tapped a thermometer hanging from a centre pillar. 'Seventy degrees constant. We've three main types of greenhouses – ordinary, the dry houses, and the store huts. The store huts are for forcing on young stuff – can't show you one right now, though. They're being restocked, which is a pretty chaotic business.' He gave a sudden scowl. 'About this time last year some kids crossed over from Kenbeg and broke into this hut and a couple of others. They fooled around, left doors open, heaters switched off, fitments damaged. Then they got clean away – and the same night there was a hard frost. You know what it cost me? A probable five thousand pounds profit. So now I make sure I know who's coming ashore, day or night – and it pays.'

'You use patrols?'

'Well, that's maybe overstating. Call them night watchmen. They've caught one or two prowlers to date, but what matters most is that the word has gone out that Buidhe is off limits for outsiders.'

Carrick touched one of the cactus plants, feeling the spikey, hard skin it was already developing. 'They'd see any boats going up or down the channel by night?'

'Probably. They didn't see the *Mora* the night she vanished, if that's what you mean.'

'I'd like to talk to them.'

'Now?' Tenford grimaced. 'All right, the two night men should be up and around by now. Wait here and I'll see what I can do.' Then, at an afterthought, he chuckled. 'You'll be cooler outside.'

The mild October air was a welcome comfort. Carrick stood outside the glass structure while Tenford hurried off, pipe clenched between his teeth. While he waited, a couple of men went past, one wheeling a barrow. They were small, muscular individuals, unshaven, who gave him a brief, formal nod of greeting as they went on their way.

Hands in his pockets, Carrick strolled a few steps towards the next greenhouse, looked through the glass at the high, broad-stemmed plants, then with a sudden feeling he was being watched, spun round on his heel.

For a moment he glimpsed a face peering at him through the glass of the greenhouse he'd just left. Then it had gone – but it was a face he'd seen before, the same truculent jaw, an impression of greasy overalls below. Farley, the man who'd met him at the landing stage, might be the island's mechanic. But he seemed to take a particular interest in Buidhe's visitors. Carrick froze for a moment, then casually, deliberately, continued strolling around as if nothing had happened.

Robert Tenford returned in another couple of minutes. With him was a lanky young man with a hard mouth and long, dark, neatly combed hair. He wore an incongruous outfit of heavy boots and overalls with a gaily patterned shirt and a wrinkled silk cravat.

'This is Tommy Vanden, one of our night men,' said Tenford. 'He's all yours.'

'Thanks.' Carrick measured the youngster, choosing his words. 'Vanden, what's your normal spell on duty?'

'Eight at night till around six a.m.' Vanden eyed him warily. 'Why? If it's about that fishing boat –'

'The *Mora*?' Carrick shook his head. 'Mr Tenford told me you didn't see her. But what about other craft – any other craft you can remember on Monday or Tuesday night?'

'Well –' Vanden frowned and glanced towards Tenford. The bulb-grower ran one hand through his thinning grey hair and his voice boomed, urging Vanden on.

'Let's have it, Tommy. We haven't all day.'

'Aye.' Vanden sucked his lips. 'Well, Monday night there were one or two fishing boats comin' in – none going out. Our own boat, the drifter, sailed in around eight – I'd just started a patrol, and that big catamaran the *Gooshgash* was headin' out to sea at the same time.'

'When did she get back?' asked Carrick, holding his voice quiet and level.

'Late on, about two in the morning.'

'Usual navigation lights?'

'That time, yes – but she didn't on the Tuesday.'

'Now wait a moment . . .' Robert Tenford chewed hard on his pipestem. 'What's this all about, Carrick?'

'Give me a couple more questions. Vanden, what about Tuesday night? When did the catamaran leave?'

Vanden shuffled his feet and looked towards Tenford. 'Around ten at night – she was close into our side of the channel when she went out. She was showin' lights then all right.'

'And when she came back?'

'That was around four a.m. –' Vanden gave an awkward grin – 'no lights, an' using sail only.'

'Any idea who was on board?'

The youngster shook his head. 'Nope. It was pretty dark. What were they up to anyway?'

Tenford growled, his patience exhausted. 'That's all, Tommy. Better get back to whatever you were doing.' He let the youngster walk out of earshot then scowled at Carrick. 'What the hell are you trying to pull on John Page? If you're trying to tie him in with that drunk MacPherson or with what happened to the *Thrift* –'

'I'm trying to find out why too many people around these islands are scared of the truth.' Carrick met his glare, his face iron-hard, a chill edge to the words. 'What about you, Mr Tenford? Did you know Page was taking his catamaran out on those late-night jaunts?'

'No, and if I'd known what you were after –' Tenford's mouth shut like a trap for a moment, then his manner changed. 'Look, there's plenty of possible explanations.'

'Then we'll find them.' Carrick looked at his wristwatch. 'Doctor Perris should be through by now. Mind if we head back to the landing stage?'

'Whatever you want,' said Tenford wearily.

'Oh, and thanks for the tour.'

'Pleasure.' It came with a cynical grimace.

They walked back to the shore in silence. The same greasy-overalled mechanic was there, tinkering with the speedboat's engine.

'Doctor Perris anywhere around, Farley?' asked Tenford.

'Along the shore.' Farley used a spanner as a pointer. The physician was already coming towards them, stepping nimbly over the rocks, his medical bag in one hand.

'All set,' he greeted them cheerfully. 'Bob, your fellow's fixed up. I've left some penicillin tablets and a written note about changing dressings. Give him a few days' light duties and that should do it.'

'Good.' Tenford seemed relieved. 'You'll be back?'

Doctor Perris raised one bushy eyebrow. 'Well, if that's a social invitation, yes. I'm not planning to leave until morning. What do you have in mind?'

'Dinner, tonight.' Tenford's face hardened as he turned to Carrick. 'There's work waiting, so I'll say goodbye. But remember, I don't take kindly to friends being hounded without reason.'

He waited on the landing stage while Carrick and the doctor boarded the pack-boat. Then, as it growled away, blunt nose pointing towards Kenbeg, Carrick had a last glimpse of the owner of Buidhe walking stiff-backed towards the shore.

'Had a spot of bother?' Doctor Perris gave a faint grin when there was no answer, then settled back near the bow, his black bag between his legs, one hand trailing lightly through the water.

Carrick took out a cigarette, cupped his hands to shield the lighter's flame, then took a long, lung-filling draw of the smoke. With that house, the bulb plots, those greenhouses and the rest Robert Tenford seemed to have a pretty profitable setup.

But why the guard on the landing stage, the guard who'd first followed him around then apparently attached himself to Doctor Perris? He might be a mechanic, but back there at the landing stage he'd been eager to make himself look busy. Too eager – otherwise why should he have been trying to fit a carburettor on upside down?

Lunch aboard *Marlin* was a grim, thoughtful gathering with one place empty at the wardroom table. The two county policemen and Campbell, the bank official, had accepted Captain Shannon's invitation. But Doctor Perris, after the usual introductions, had called for a ham sandwich and a bottle of beer – then had disappeared into the cruiser's tiny, stripped-down sickbay to get down to his post-mortem examination.

92

'So now we've got Page on the list as well as Sawny MacKenna – and not a chance of anyone on Kenbeg even giving us the time of day without contacting MacKenna first. Damn these close-mouthed islanders!' Chief Inspector Dawe frowned down at his plate, much to the annoyance of the hovering steward. Porterhouse steak wasn't served every day aboard *Marlin*, and when it was, he expected it to be treated with respect.

Carrick gave a slight shrug. 'They're pretty loyal on the islands –'

'Loyal?' The detective made it sound indecent. 'Tight-mouthed, conniving, double-dealing . . . you should have seen MacKenna in here a little while back. Oh, he'd just heard about MacPherson's body being found. What a terrible thing it was, and if there was anything he could do to help, then all we had to do was tell him. So I asked him again where he'd been on Monday and Tuesday night. And got the same story as before, that he'd been sitting out at his oyster farm with a shotgun on his knees.'

Carrick carved another forkful from his steak. 'He doesn't know about Jean MacPherson's story – that she saw the catamaran on Tuesday night?'

'No. But now that we've got confirmation from this night watchman the time's almost ripe to bring it out in the open. Just give me long enough to settle a couple of other details and then I'll tackle John Page – while Sergeant Wylie takes a shorthand note. Let a man try to lie his way out of a situation, have him tell the same story a few times over, and he usually crumbles. It's a damned difficult thing to be a consistent liar. Sawny MacKenna may have the gift, but I'll bank on Page being more of an amateur.'

Across the table, Henry Campbell laid down his knife and fork, then wiped his moustache with his table napkin. 'From the bank's viewpoint, I'm concerned about the *Thrift*.'

'Eh?' Captain Shannon came to life with a start. 'What about her?'

'Well ...' Campbell waited until the steward had whisked away his plate. 'The boat is sea-worthy, there's that money aboard and having it out of service is an embarrassment to the bank.'

'An embarrassment!' Shannon made it a savage bark. 'Three men missing and more than likely dead, yet you talk about embarrassment!'

Campbell paled. 'I'm still a servant of the bank, Captain. I know young Sword, our clerk, is your nephew. But it also happens that I was an apprentice with John Wilson, the same Wilson who was the manager aboard her. All I'm trying to say is that the *Thrift* can't lie moored here indefinitely.'

'It won't.' Chief Inspector Dawe silenced them both. 'If I can borrow a couple of men from your crew, Captain, I'm going to have Sergeant Wylie sail back with it to the mainland.'

'And who's going to tow her?' demanded Shannon. 'She's sea-worthy, yes. But her engine needs to be stripped down and overhauled before it'll run again.'

'Hmm.' The policeman frowned, considering. 'I'm not interested in banking problems. But I want that boat back within reach of decent forensic facilities, where we can take the thing to pieces if we have to – if there's any pointer to what happened hidden aboard, I want to find it.'

Captain Shannon shot a vindictive glance towards the bank official. 'That's different. I can put some of my engineroom squad to work on her. Give them the rest of the day and they should have her in some sort of shape.' He rubbed his chin. 'Still, she'd better have an escort in case of breakdowns.'

Sergeant Wylie, a silent spectator so far, stopped buttering a biscuit and leaned forward. 'Why not try this fellow Tenford? That drifter of his could do the job.'

'And tow it all the way if necessary,' agreed Dawe. 'Well, Captain?'

'It sounds fine,' agreed Shannon. He glanced at Carrick. 'What's wrong, mister. You don't seem to like the idea.'

Carrick shrugged. 'It couldn't do much harm, I suppose.'

'Still worried about the reception you got on Buidhe?' Dawe gave a grunt. 'So Tenford doesn't like strangers and has one or two private police to keep an eye on his property – well, that's no crime. We've already checked on him. Right, Sergeant?'

Sergeant Wylie nodded. 'Good financial background, no record, generally rated as a solid citizen, and half of the local population ready to confirm his drifter didn't leave the bay between Sunday and today.'

'We've one or two tastier titbits,' said Dawe, dismissing the matter. 'For instance, we've had a reply on that check round mainland buyers. It seems Drammy MacPherson's been making a habit of dipping lobster creels that didn't belong to him. They weren't keen on admitting it, but we've found three buyers who've been doing business with him for long enough. Never a lot involved, but it would all add up to quite a little nest-egg.'

'But does it matter?' asked Campbell. The bank investigator glanced cautiously towards Shannon. 'All this talk about MacPherson probably has no connection with the *Thrift*.'

'That's on my mind too.' Dawe pushed back his chair and rose to his feet. 'Any objection if I get your radioman to send another message, Captain?'

Shannon shook his head. 'Do what you want.'

'Fine. I want to tell Headquarters to get a move on with that background report on John Page. Even if his family do own a hotel, running a boat like that catamaran costs money. I'd like to know just how Mr Page gets his money – from what I've gathered, the vet bills he collects wouldn't keep him in beer money.' He gave a small, cold smile. 'Anyway, you can relax now, Captain Shannon. Fishery Protection's done a pretty good job, but I think we can take care of the rest.'

Shannon sat still as his guests departed. But as Carrick made to follow them out he summoned him back with a beckoning finger.

'Sir?'

'Ever have a thing called a hunch, mister?' demanded *Marlin's* skipper abruptly.

'Sometimes.' Carrick stayed quiet, sensing the glow of anger inside the older man. Being told, however politely, that he could now mind his own business was no diplomatic way to deal with the small, red-faced Superintendent of Fisheries.

The fingers of Shannon's right hand drummed on the table for a moment. 'Then I've one now – that our two policemen are too confident for their own good. I think you should stretch your legs a little. Take a walk along the coast to this oyster farm of MacKenna's, for a start – better take Petty Officer Bell with you, just in case you need a witness. On the way back –' he pursed his lips – 'well, that's your business. I'm maybe close to retiral age, but I'm still fairly well aware of what's going on around me. You've got either something or someone on your mind, Carrick. Don't go tripping over our policemen, but stay with it.'

A brisk twenty-minute walk from the village and out across the grassy central spine of Kenbeg Island brought Carrick and Clapper Bell to its north-east shore, a place of high cliffs, screaming seabirds and long, white-crested waves. The wind tugging at their clothing, they moved along the edge of the cliffs at a more leisurely pace, scanning each little cove and bay in turn.

'Hell, there'd be nothin' funny in taking a tumble from here,' said Clapper Bell, a frown creasing his leathery face as he looked down yet another sheer drop to the tangle of rocks at its base. 'There's damn all plastic about that stuff.'

Carrick nodded, noticing the small colonies of gulls perched here and there on narrow, crack-like ledges. He thought of the scar on Arran MacKenna's hand. Scrambling down a rope in search of gulls' eggs could be a chancy business in a place like this – even for a youngster in search of pocket money. Anyway, gulls' eggs were one alleged delicacy he'd never appreciated. 'Let's try farther on.'

Beyond the next little headland they struck lucky, a faint trace of a pathway leading down a steep decline. They scrambled down it, and found themselves in a hidden, well-sheltered cove, little more than a split in the rocks around. At sea-level, the beach was a mixture of sand-silted shingle. But a little way back just on high-water mark lay a stretch of bare, living rock, its centre worn away by some freak of nature's past to form a saucer-like pool. All around were traces of Sawny MacKenna's labours.

Loose shingle and weed had been cleared away. A wooden sluice-gate sat in the middle of a foot-high wall of cemented stones which ran across the mouth of the pool. It was enough to bar the sweep of tidal water, yet the sluice-gate would allow for drainage and refilling as required.

'Plenty o' them anyway,' muttered Bell, looking into the shallow pool. At first glance, the oyster shells, many of them bearing young white spat, lay close enough together to have all the appearance of a thick carpet laid over the rock.

Carrick moved round the edge of the pool, picking a few samples at random. When he returned, he shook his head. 'Dead, every last one of them. I'll take a couple back as samples.'

'So old MacKenna was tellin' the truth this time.' Clapper Bell grinned. 'Makes a change. What now, sir?'

97

'Better take a look around while we're here.' He turned his back on the pool and began crunching over the shingle, his companion falling into step.

Their first find was close under the base of the cliffs, a few hand-tools wrapped in sacking and stowed in a sheltered overhang. Then, as they moved on again, Clapper Bell suddenly gripped him by the arm.

'There's a wee hut or somethin' up the back there. See it? Beside that boulder like a ruddy tombstone slab.'

Carrick followed his pointing finger and nodded. The hut was little more than a low shelter built of driftwood. They must have practically walked past it on their way down.

'I'll take a look.' He started towards the shelter, moving cautiously over the loose rocks. What happened next he wasn't sure – Clapper Bell's shout of warning, the flicker of movement from the shelter itself, or the orange muzzle-flash and blast of the gun, the sound magnified by the cliffs around. The bullet whipped past his head as he threw himself sideways behind the nearest boulders, thudding down against the hard jagged shingle.

A second shot roared while the echo of the first still played against the cliffs, sending scores of seabirds screaming into the air. Hugging the beach, Carrick edged himself round and looked back. Clapper Bell had similarly vanished from sight. Then he saw him, wriggling forward from one rock shelter to the next. Someone else saw the bo'sun at the same moment – two more shots blasted out in quick succession, sparking chips from the rocks as Bell made a frantic dive back where he'd come from, then adding their wild, whining ricochet to the chorus of noise.

Then, suddenly, it was quiet. Carrick lay where he was, muscles tensed. The marksman could be playing it coolly, waiting there for a clear view of his targets. Or he might be retreating – but either way, there was no dividend in volunteering for a hole in the head.

A full minute ticked past on his wristwatch, then, as the second hand swept round again, he reached out, lifted a large, round pebble, and tossed it over to his left. It landed with a clatter – but there was no reaction. He stayed where he was for a few more seconds, the shingle beneath him pressing harsh against his flesh, before he finally raised himself a few inches from shelter.

Nothing happened. He stood up, dusted himself down with one hand, and gave a twisted smile as Clapper Bell loped towards him. There was a trickle of blood running down the bo'sun's face from a small gash on his forehead.

'A ruddy stone-chip splinter,' he said ruefully. 'An' I never even got to see the bloke.'

'At that we're maybe lucky.' Carrick took another cautious look around. 'Well, he's probably far away by now. Let's see why he was so anxious to keep from meeting us.'

The hut, when they reached it, was a tumbledown makeshift. Inside, it was empty apart from a couple of old wooden boxes.

'Maybe he just didn't like us,' declared Clapper Bell, squatting down and peering around. 'Still, here's somethin'.' His hand reached out and he held up a small brass cartridge case. 'For my money it's from an automatic, a .38.'

Carrick nodded grimly. 'Which could mean we nearly met the same character who used a gun on the *Thrift*. Keep looking, Clapper.'

They located two more of the little brass cylinders, lying outside among the rocks. But while they were still searching for the fourth, Carrick made a different discovery – one which made Sawny MacKenna's situation more precarious than ever.

The oilskin package had been hidden in a hollow under a broad flat stone. But as the edge of Carrick's foot clipped the stone it moved free and betrayed its secret. He stooped, opened the wrapping, and felt a sharp pang of mixed anger and despair – anger at what lay in his hands, despair at what it might mean to MacKenna's two grey-eyed daughters.

'For the luv o' –' Clapper Bell swallowed. 'That stuff beats oyster farmin' any time!'

There was, at a rough count, over seven hundred pounds in the roll of paper money, all in new, uncreased fives. Carrick folded the oilskin round it again, and shoved the package in his pocket.

'Let's go, Clapper,' he said slowly. 'Let's find out if MacKenna's at home.'

They headed back, Carrick's mind in a bitter turmoil. But there was an anti-climax waiting when they reached the cottage in the village. Despite Clapper Bell's repeated hammering knock on the door there was no reply.

Carrick tried the handle. It turned easily – in the Hebrides there's still an old-fashioned belief that it isn't polite to lock people out of your house, isn't necessary to guard against thieves when each man is your neighbour.

'Eh ... are we goin' in?' asked Bell uneasily. 'Look, it's still daylight an' we've no search warrant or anythin' like that.'

'Worried?' Carrick raised a surprised eyebrow.

'Aye. There's a woman headin' this way from the next cottage, an' she's not the friendly type.'

She reached them a moment later, stout, middle-aged, a heavy shawl wrapped round her shoulders. 'You're from the Fishery Protection.' It was question, statement, and distrust rolled into one.

'From *Marlin*,' agreed Carrick.

'Well, you can bang on that door as long as you like but there's nobody at home,' she told them, pulling the shawl tight. 'Mr MacKenna and the girls have gone out – the girls asked me to keep an eye open for folk arriving.'

'Any idea where they are?' Carrick switched to a mild, friendly smile.

'Mr MacKenna's away out on one o' the boats.' The woman didn't thaw. 'The girls are away over to Jean

100

MacPherson's, though it's no welcome they'll find there.' She stepped determinedly between them and the door, her arms folded. 'So there's no sense in you staying, is there?'

'None,' agreed Carrick. He glanced sideways at Clapper Bell. But for once even the bo'sun's usual determination had dried up.

From the cottage, Carrick set a fast pace towards the fishery cruiser. But when he got aboard, neither Chief Inspector Dawe nor Sergeant Wylie were in sight.

'They've gone ashore,' Captain Shannon told him, gnawing his lip as he stared down at the bundle of money lying on the wardroom table. 'I'll send a messenger – then it's up to them what they do.'

'Not much option, I'd say.' Doctor Perris, a large whisky in one hand, a cigarette in the other, stood across the table. 'Sawny MacKenna's got a lot of explaining to do – if he can.' He took a long swallow from his glass. 'At least my job's done. A simple, uncomplicated drowning, if you leave the alcohol aspect out of the picture.'

'You're sure?' Carrick stared at him in surprise.

'Positive. Death was probably two days ago, though with a drowning it's hard to be precise. The rest – well there were the usual internal conditions.'

'But the way he was tangled up in that lobster creel, with no lobster and no bait –'

'You wouldn't be suggesting I don't know my job, Carrick?' Doctor Perris' smile changed to a frown, the bushy eyebrows merging on his forehead in almost comical fashion. 'Now listen, young fellow, I've probably had more drowning autopsies on my plate over the years than you've had hot dinners. Any second year student could have settled this one – water in the stomach, oedematous condition of the lungs, absolutely no sign of external injury during life.' He snorted. 'Because of the fuss going on, I chemical-checked the blood – and I'll want an extra fee for that, I can tell you.'

'Check?' Carrick looked towards Captain Shannon, still reluctant to accept the verdict. 'What for?'

'Blood chloride,' snapped the doctor, indignation growing. 'Water entering the lungs when a man's drowning passes to the left side of the heart. If it's salt water, it steps up the chloride content of the blood. MacPherson's content was up forty per cent. The only other thing worth noting was that he'd a fair whack of liquor in his gut. Satisfied?'

'Dawe is,' growled Captain Shannon. 'He's gone with Sergeant Wylie to tell Jean MacPherson the result, though they won't release his body straight away. They're moving it to a cold-store shed in the village for another couple of days – usual routine, nothing more to it now.'

Perris growled agreement. 'And after that they're planning to pick up John Page, correct?'

Shannon nodded. 'Soon as they can. Mister, we've had a radio message from a Norwegian cargo ship, the *Velella* – she picked up the general request message put out by Oban Radio. According to the *Velella* she passed a catamaran yacht just north of the Abbey Isles late on Tuesday night. The sighting was logged, because the catamaran was running without lights.

'The Abbey Isles, mister – they're uninhabited, they've been checked by those lobstermen looking for MacPherson, and I took a look at them myself yesterday. But they're in the area where the *Thrift* could have been that night, and not much more than ten miles from Black Reef light.'

Chapter Five

Once delivered, Captain Shannon's message brought Chief Inspector Dawe and his sergeant back to the harbour and *Marlin's* wardroom in double-quick time . . . but they came alone.

'We missed them,' growled Dawe, his thin, angular face showing disappointment. 'According to Mrs MacPherson, Page and one of the MacKenna girls left minutes before we arrived. Still, we collected Drammy's bank passbook – and a couple of canisters of rat poison, both near enough to empty. They were hidden in the boat's hull, among the rubbish near the bow.'

'No need to ask where they were used,' mused Captain Shannon. 'Old hate dies hard, and young MacPherson was raised on a pretty steady diet of it. But MacKenna has a shock coming when he hears who wiped out his oysters.'

'Does it matter?' Dawe frowned down at the banknotes on the wardroom table. 'Page's catamaran is still in the bay, so I'll take it he's ashore somewhere.' He glanced towards Carrick. 'But MacKenna worries me. This woman you spoke to – how do you know she wasn't lying?'

'I don't,' said Carrick laconically, trying to control his growing dislike of the man. 'But the lobster boats are out, and MacKenna could be on any of them.'

'Well, when he comes back we nail him.' Dawe settled himself into a chair. 'Where's our banking expert?'

'On the *Thrift*,' said Captain Shannon. 'Doctor Perris has taken a dinghy over to bring him back – oh, and he said he'd get down to the official PM report as soon as he could.'

'Good.' Dawe rubbed a hand across his face. 'Then let's have that bo'sun of yours in, Captain. The sooner we sort out this little lot the better.'

Clapper Bell answered the summons. For the next ten minutes he and Carrick found themselves being grilled by a gradually triumphant Dawe while Sergeant Wylie's pencil and notebook fought to keep pace. Halfway through, Henry Campbell arrived, was given a brief explanation, then retired into a corner with the banknotes and began thumbing through them one by one.

The questioning went on.

'You're both sure about this – neither of you saw who was doing the shooting, hadn't even the barest impression?' persisted Dawe for what seemed the tenth time running.

'I didn't, and for ruddy good reason,' rumbled Clapper Bell unabashed. 'I don't mind doin' folk favours, but the notion o' stickin' my head up above those boulders would have been damn silly.' He touched the cut on his forehead with tender care. 'The bloke was tryin' hard, that's all I know.'

'You, Carrick?'

Carrick gave a weary shake of his head. 'I've already told you.'

'Not quite everything,' said Dawe, leaning forward. 'What reason took you to that oyster farm in the first place?'

'Curiosity,' said Carrick wooden-faced. 'It paid off, didn't it?'

Dawe grunted. 'Let's find out. Campbell?'

The bank investigator sucked his thin moustache and nodded. 'All these notes are from the *Thrift*, Chief Inspector. They total roughly half the amount missing – and I'd say the rest would probably have been paid out in normal customer transactions before the raid.'

'We've got men checking on that,' grunted Dawe. He got up and prowled the wardroom impatiently. 'Right. We want MacKenna and Page, and it would do no harm to have a talk with MacKenna's daughters while we're at it. Any of them could have fired these shots – and I'm ninety-nine per cent positive the cartridge firing pin markings will tie them in with the gun used on the bank boat.' He ticked points off one by one on his fingers. 'The money's found at MacKenna's oyster farm, we've got witnesses that Page's catamaran sneaked out of here on Monday night then Tuesday night – two nights when MacKenna has an alibi as weak as a paper bag. That adds up to one answer.'

'You sound pretty certain,' murmured Carrick, looking through the wardroom porthole and out across the bay. 'Would it be an answer able to stand up in court?'

'Not yet, but that'll come.' The detective nodded towards Sergeant Wylie and the latter closed his notebook with weary relief. 'The bits and pieces are coming together, Carrick – that's what I meant by investigation routine. Page, for instance. His family have the hotel he talks about. But I've a report in about our Mr Page. He doesn't get his money from there, and nobody's quite sure where it does come from.' He slammed one fist against the other. 'I know what you're thinking, Carrick – that I'm pushing the pace. All right, I am. But I've got a Chief Constable snapping at my heels, with Campbell's bank sharpening their claws on him in the background.'

Carrick nodded, still looking out across the bay. 'You've got your troubles, Chief Inspector. But maybe you're pushing too hard and too soon.'

'I'm not – and when MacKenna's boat comes in I'll prove it.'

'Fine.' Carrick swung round from the porthole. 'Then you'd better get out on that pier. The lobster boats are coming in.'

Captain Shannon beat the two detectives to the porthole by a short head, peered out, and saw for himself. Four boats were coming into the bay, growing larger every moment. Overhead, the sky was dull and grey – and that same greyness seemed to spread to Shannon as the lead boat came closer and he recognized the tall, white-haired figure standing at her bow.

'There he is, Chief Inspector,' said *Marlin's* captain with a strange, grim reluctance. 'While you're collecting him, I'll send a shore patrol to locate Page.'

They marched Sawny MacKenna aboard the fishery cruiser a few minutes later. He was protesting noisily, one arm waving emphasis to his words, the other held firm by Sergeant Wylie. Chief Inspector Dawe followed a step or two behind, listening to it all with something close to a grin.

On deck, MacKenna glared as he came face to face with Captain Shannon, then launched on a new tirade.

'What is it this time, eh?' He tugged at Wylie's restraining grip and snarled. 'Captain or no captain, I'll finish you for this, Shannon – you and these two thickheads of policemen. Oh, there's ways of causing a row, my wee Superintendent of Fisheries – and I'll damned well use every one of them!'

For once Shannon stayed silent, merely jerking his head towards the companionway. Wylie gave his prisoner a push and they went below, MacKenna's voice still echoing up long after they'd disappeared.

'Picked him up as he stepped ashore,' said Chief Inspector Dawe happily. 'Oh, and I saw your men heading for the village. Thanks.'

'They'll do what they can.' Shannon beckoned towards Carrick. 'Better come along with me, mister.'

'To keep the odds even, eh? Two of us and two of you?' Dawe's face held a bubbling expectancy.

106

'As far as I know, we're on the same side,' said Shannon softly. 'If MacKenna killed my nephew then I'll have only one regret ... that I can't strangle the life out of him with my own hands.' He swung on his heel and led the way.

Marlin's steward, like many another man aboard, was ex-Royal Navy – and from a memory of some distant court-martial he'd used what time was available to arrange the wardroom accordingly. Covered by a laundered white cloth, a long table sat across most of the width of the cabin. Two chairs were behind it, one for his captain and the other for Chief Inspector Dawe. In front, separated by a few feet of space, another chair was placed on its own for the prisoner.

Quieter now, a more worried look gradually spreading over his face, Sawny MacKenna watched Shannon and the detective take their places. A nudge from Sergeant Wylie, and he followed their example. Wylie glanced questioningly towards Clapper Bell then, as the bo'sun nodded and took over behind MacKenna, he moved aside and produced the same notebook, holding his pencil ready over a fresh page.

'Now then –' Chief Inspector Dawe leaned forward, his clasped hands resting on the table – 'MacKenna, we've talked before. But this time I'm starting with a formal caution. Anything you say –'

'I've plenty to say, believe me!' grated MacKenna.

'Good. Then it may be taken down in writing and used in evidence.' Dawe rattled through the inevitable formula and bared his teeth in a narrow-lipped smile. 'MacKenna, I'm going to give you four facts and save you the trouble of lying – and us the trouble of listening to you lying. We've witnesses who saw the catamaran *Gooshgash* leave here early on Monday evening and come back in at a late hour. We've other witnesses who saw the *Gooshgash* leave here on Tuesday night, come back in without lights at four a.m., then sneak out again. We've a report

107

which places a catamaran off the Abbey Isles on Tuesday midnight – again without lights.' He reached into his coat pocket and tossed the bundle of banknotes on the table between them. 'We've these. Seven hundred and fifty pounds, found at your oyster farm. The numbers show they came from the *Thrift*.' He clasped his hands once more. 'Well, MacKenna?'

Sawny MacKenna had stiffened in his chair, his eyes fixed on the banknotes. When he looked up, it was to Shannon while the tip of his tongue ran delicately over his lips. 'Now that you mention it, maybe there's a thing or two I forgot about.'

'Like why somebody – either Page or one of your daughters – tried to shoot the men who found the money?' grated Dawe.

'Damn that for a lie!' MacKenna heaved up from the chair, to be rammed back down again as Clapper Bell's massive hands landed one on each of his shoulders. 'Who says it?'

'We were shot at, Sawny,' confirmed Carrick, sitting with his back against the curve of the ship's side. His lips tightened for an instant as he glanced towards Dawe. 'But we don't know who was behind the gun.'

Dawe flushed. 'That doesn't mean we're completely in the dark. What about the rest of it, MacKenna?'

'Aye, I was warned it would come to this.' Sawny MacKenna spoke half to himself, half to the others in the cabin. 'And I was right, like I said it would happen. You really think I did it, don't you?'

'MacKenna –' The detective stopped with an irritated frown as Captain Shannon laid a hand on his arm. 'All right, try if you want, Captain.'

Shannon stroked his short spade beard for a moment. 'This isn't a trial, Sawny.'

'Then it has most of the trappings,' said MacKenna bleakly. 'And a verdict in advance, by the look of things.'

'If you've a story tell it,' urged Shannon uncomfortably. 'Man, if it's true and you're innocent nobody will suffer – you have my word for it.'

'Young Sword was your nephew and you want blood for him.' MacKenna shrugged and put his hands deep in his trouser pockets. 'Well, why not? Any man would. But my girls have no part in this . . . understood?' He looked around him, and, though not one of them spoke, seemed to find what he wanted in their faces. 'John Page's boat was out when you say, and the money's mine.'

Across the table, Chief Inspector Dawe's mouth showed his surprise. 'You admit it?'

'That much, but no more. Not about the *Thrift*, not about whoever was shooting at Mr Carrick – I'd no part in these things.'

'Then tell us why you were out in the cat,' challenged Carrick, watching the fisherman through narrowed eyelids. There was a strangely confident air about MacKenna now, the air of a man, who, a decision taken, was tasting the relief brought with it.

'My daughter Aline marries John Page next month – you know that.' MacKenna leaned back in his chair. 'I had a good notion where the bank boat would be lying on Monday night. They usually lie over at Cliad Bay, on the west side of Coll first night out. So I got John to take me down there on his *Gooshgash*. We met the *Thrift*, I drew seven hundred and fifty pounds from my savings account, and John brought me home again.'

Sergeant Wylie stopped writing and gave a gurgle of disbelief. Then, as Dawe glared at him, he began scribbling at top speed.

'You drew seven hundred and fifty!' Dawe's voice dripped sarcasm. 'Why the rush? Why not wait until the *Thrift* reached here on the Wednesday?'

'Because I had an arrangement which was put forward a bit and I needed the money.' MacKenna looked blandly around him. 'When a man's daughter is married, a man has to have enough refreshment in the place for the wedding feast. I needed two hundred pounds for that. Five hundred of the rest I was putting aside as a present for Aline's wedding day, and the other fifty was to be for Arran.'

'Two hundred –' Dawe swallowed hard. 'You expect to get away with a yarn like that? For two hundred quid I could damned near stock a pub!'

'For an island wedding it is appropriate,' said the fisherman with a sudden, stiff dignity.

'He's right,' said Captain Shannon with a faint wisp of a smile. 'I've been at an island wedding, Dawe. Five days and five nights they'll last – and the bride's parents insulted if there's a man fit to walk at the end.' He traced a vague pattern on the tablecloth with his thumbnail. 'And this arrangement, Sawny – a special arrangement, with a fishing boat coming over from Ireland perhaps? And nobody bothering about customs formalities or the like?'

An answering twinkle lighted in MacKenna's eyes. 'A wedding can be expensive, and a man with two daughters must make his arrangements.'

'But your arrangement was put forward to the Tuesday night off the Abbey Isles?' Carrick hesitated for a moment, fascinated, trying hard to decide whether the story was as wild as it sounded. He'd heard men speak in near awe of the few places in the Hebrides where the old tradition was still maintained, strongholds where a wedding meant a week of celebration with a month's hangover to follow. For that week an hour or two's sleep was thought enough to keep any true man going – and the fact that bride and groom were long departed on their honeymoon had little bearing on the matter.

'Ach, he radioed he'd have to bring the stuff three nights early,' confirmed MacKenna. He removed one hand from a pocket and scratched under one arm. 'I had to get the money in a hurry, this friend of mine liking cash on the barrel, so to speak. John took me down on his boat

110

on the Monday because it has twice the speed of anything around here. Then my own damn boat disappears, and I have to ask him to help me out on the Tuesday night – only the stupid fool of an Irishman didn't show up at all.'

'Just like that.' Chief Inspector Dawe snapped his fingers in something close to grudging admiration, then tenderly, almost lovingly, played his trump card. 'And of course the *Thrift's* records would show you'd drawn the money – if someone in a frogman suit hadn't stolen them once she was brought into Kenbeg.' His voice changed to a growl. 'MacKenna, maybe you did have some crazy reason for going on the *Thrift* on Monday night. Maybe that's when you found she was carrying a load of extra cash – or much more likely you had this raid planned from the start, couldn't find her on the Monday night and tried again on the Tuesday.'

'But I've been telling you –'

'I'll do the telling,' snapped Dawe. 'You and Page raided the *Thrift* then took fright when you opened the safe and found the notes were brand new. But you couldn't resist taking a bundle, could you? Who used the gun on her crew, MacKenna?'

'We weren't there.' MacKenna threw him a stubborn glance.

'Captain?' Carrick caught Shannon's eye, received a brief nod, and walked over to stand beside the fisherman. 'Who took the bank records from the *Thrift*, Sawny?'

MacKenna shrugged. 'I did. If you'd found them the police would have done this to me just that little bit sooner.'

'Where are they?'

'Burned, and my passbook with them.'

'Because you were scared?' Carrick watched him closely. 'Suppose even part of this story was true, Sawny. There's another reason why you'd want those records, isn't there? Once they were destroyed you'd be left with the money and no record of it being drawn from your account.'

111

Dawe gave a cynical smile. 'That sounds better, but I'm still not swallowing it.'

MacKenna avoided their gaze. 'Believe what you like. But they're gone – and I dumped the frogman gear out at sea.'

'So it's gone too,' said Carrick mildly. 'Well now, was there an air safety reserve valve on your tanks?'

The man moistened his lips then nodded.

'How did you recharge the tanks – with the reserve lever up or down?'

'Eh ... up.'

'Here's something else any diver would know. What's the exposure time limit at a hundred feet – twenty-five minutes or thirty-five?'

'Thirty-five.'

'Wrong both times.' Carrick shook his head. 'As a diver you're a washout, Sawny.'

'I've said all I'm going to without a lawyer,' declared MacKenna bitterly. 'If you're going to charge me, let's get it over with.'

'Let's say you're staying aboard to help us with inquiries,' said Dawe grimly. 'You've somewhere we can keep him, Captain Shannon?'

Shannon nodded. 'There's a spare storeroom. I can put a guard on the door.'

'Fine,' grated Dawe. 'And don't worry about the charge, MacKenna. It'll come, once I've had a talk with John Page. You wouldn't like to tell me where he is – or where your girls are, come to that?'

Sawny MacKenna's eyes narrowed for a moment and he seemed about to speak. But he shrugged instead, gave a slow shake of his head, and rose to his feet.

The rest of the afternoon dragged on under a dull grey sky. Chief Inspector Dawe searched the MacKenna cottage and Page's catamaran without success. *Marlin's* shore patrol

112

returned, reported failure, and were sent straight out again. But Carrick couldn't complain of having time on his hands. Once MacKenna had been led away Captain Shannon first disappeared to the bridge then returned with a list of ship-keeping jobs for immediate attention – deck department jobs, maintenance and stores routines which kept both Carrick and Jumbo Wills hard at work until after dusk.

At last, as lights began to twinkle from behind a score of cottage curtains over in the night-shrouded village, Carrick found himself free. Tired and grimy, he headed for his cabin, treated himself to the luxury of a shower and a clean shirt, then began running his electric razor over the darkening stubble on his cheeks.

Halfway through, he heard a peremptory double knock on the cabin door. As he switched off the razor the door swung open and Captain Shannon looked in. Shannon stood where he was for a moment, a tight expression on his face, then entered, closing the door behind him.

'I want a word with you, Webb.'

First-name terms from Shannon were as clear a warning as any storm cone. Carrick swept a bundle of magazines from the cabin's only chair. As Shannon lowered himself into it, he perched on the edge of the bunk, waiting.

'What do you think of MacKenna's story?' asked Shannon abruptly.

'It's pretty wild, but –'

'But it could be true. A man caught up in his own little maze of lying. Your idea about the bank records could be the reason for all he's done.' Shannon refused the cigarette Carrick offered, cleared his throat, and looked almost awkwardly towards the ceiling. 'You showed he was still lying when it came to the scuba gear. But what does that mean? Only that he's covering up – and I think you've a pretty good idea why?'

'The twins.' Carrick nodded, chose a cigarette, and lit it.

113

'That's how it looked. I've a feeling those girls would do most things to help their father.'

'Except this time they came unstuck.' Shannon wasn't finished. 'I don't trust the devil an inch further than I could throw him but – well, I've come near enough to admitting it, I suppose. At first when we found the *Thrift* I thought MacKenna had to be involved. Then . . . I don't know. This thing has become too much of a nightmare. This time, even though it hurts to admit it, I think most of what he said was the truth.'

'If we knew more about this Irishman he says was delivering the liquor it might help,' mused Carrick.

'I've tried asking MacKenna.' Shannon spread his hands in an unaccustomed gesture of helplessness. 'He won't name him.'

'Maybe because the Irishman doesn't exist.' Carrick drew pensively on the cigarette. 'Come to that, where have Page and the MacKenna girls hidden themselves – and why?'

'MacKenna's worried about them if nothing else. All he wanted to know from me was whether we'd located them.' Shannon scowled. 'Anyway, you're getting out of it all. That's the main reason I came. The engineroom team are back aboard and they've got the *Thrift's* clockwork running again. You'll sail her across to the mainland at first light tomorrow.'

'Any passengers, sir?'

'Henry Campbell – he insists. Depending on what happens tonight there may be others.' Shannon pursed his lips. 'I'm counting on Tenford's drifter as an escort – he'll be paid a hire fee and she's big enough to tow you if necessary. Once you've delivered at Kyle of Lochalsh the drifter will bring you back.'

Carrick nodded. 'Right. What's the weather forecast like, sir?'

'Tricky, so my advice is don't waste time. It should hold fairly steady for most of tomorrow, but after that there's all

114

the signs that we're in for a north-east gale. Anyway, I want you back aboard. Orders are we resume normal patrol within thirty-six hours.'

'We're being pulled out?'

'Official.' Shannon showed he didn't like it. 'Part of the reason may be a couple of private signals Dawe sent through our radio room this afternoon. And I gather you'll find a squad of police joining you on the drifter for the return trip.' He got up to go. 'We'll still maintain patrol in the area and be available to assist, but nothing more.'

He went out, closing the door quietly behind him. Carrick swore softly and stubbed out his cigarette on the cabin ashtray. The whole dark chain was hardening, hardening in everything except what mattered to Captain Shannon, any real lead to the fate of the missing men.

Shannon – and Arran now, Arran and her sister, Page and old Sawny. All of them were gripped by that same chain in different ways.

His broad-boned face twisted in disgust at his own helplessness. Tomorrow meant a bus-driver act across to the mainland. Tomorrow – he stopped as a thought clicked into place in his mind, then gave a sudden grin. What was wrong with tonight?

The razor hummed to life as he tackled a tricky patch of beard on his chin, a patch which might once have been a baby's dimple but was now a twice-daily hazard. He dealt with it mechanically, his mind working over the idea.

The razor had moved on to the left side of his face when another knock, soft and urgent, sounded on the door. Then it swung open. Clapper Bell nipped in, closing it fast again behind him.

'I've been hidin' roun' the corner until the Old Man got clear.' Bell grinned, a twinkle in his eyes. 'I took a walk to mysel' along the pier a minute ago an' met someone who's pretty desperate to see you.'

'Me?' Carrick raised one eyebrow in surprise, then switched off the razor.

'Uh-huh. She said –'

'One of the MacKenna girls? Arran?'

'That's the one.' Clapper Bell was enjoying himself. 'Mind you, if I'd been on that shore patrol detail I suppose I'd ha' grabbed her. But nobody gave me any orders like that.'

'She's still out there?'

'She said she'd wait.'

'Right.' Carrick glanced at his watch. 'Give me half an hour – then you and I have a little job to do, something I don't want broadcast.'

'Do we get shot at?' asked Bell warily.

'Not if we're lucky.'

'It helps to know.' The Petty Officer grunted. 'Still, what's the difference? The only other thing happening on Kenbeg tonight is a ruddy whist drive in the village hall ... an' that wouldn't have me screamin' to get in.' He watched while Carrick fastened a tie and pulled on his jacket. 'Maybe it's none o' my business, but whose side are we on?'

Carrick shrugged. He wasn't quite sure himself.

He left the *Marlin* moments later, picking a careful path along the unlit quay with its vague boobytraps of coiled lines and scattered lobster creels. Once he'd reached the sheds at the landward end he stopped, looking around.

'Webb ...' Her voice came from a few feet away. She was standing in the sheltering shadow of a high mound of fuel drums.

'We've been looking for you, Arran.' He crossed towards her, peering down at her face in the gloom, sensing as much as seeing the dark-haired girl's tightly controlled tension. 'Your father's being held on *Marlin*.'

'I know. I was warned in the village.' She gripped him tightly by the arm. 'Webb, I had to see you. It's Aline and John – I can't find them. I don't know where they are.'

116

He stood still, hearing the water lapping gently against the pier timbers. 'They could have heard about your father.'

'And are hiding?' She gave a vehement shake of her head. 'We were to meet at the cottage. We'd made up our minds to make Dad talk to Captain Shannon. But Dad was out with the boats – so Aline and John decided to see Mrs MacPherson again, and I went to the village store to get some groceries.'

'What time was this?'

'Early afternoon, before the lobster boats got back.' She bit her lip, her teeth white in the darkness. 'People kept me talking. But when I got home I could see Aline and John had been there – had been and had left again.'

'And since then?'

'I've been looking for them.' She paused. 'Looking for them and dodging your shore patrol.'

The night was cold. Carrick saw her shiver and made up his mind. 'Let's get out of here. I'll take you home.'

'But the shore patrol –'

'I'll take care of them.' Gently he freed her hand from his arm. 'Come on.'

They walked together through the rough streets of the village. Halfway along, Carrick heard other, heavier footsteps approaching and pulled her back into the shadow of a gable wall. They stayed there, close together, the warmth of her body against his, while two of Marlin's seamen strode by. Once the men had gone, Carrick grimaced to himself. He was committed now, whatever happened.

Not far from the MacKenna cottage he stopped her again. The faint glow of a shielded cigarette had caught his eye. Someone was standing in the cottage doorway.

'Arran . . .' He put his lips close to her ear. 'Give me a couple of minutes, then head round to the back.'

She nodded, then raised her head in a quick, bird-like motion. Her lips brushed his for a brief instant before she moved back, waiting.

117

Carrick drew a deep breath then marched towards the cottage, his feet crunching noisily over the pebbled path. The cigarette went out in a brief cascade of sparks and the seaman in the doorway stepped out into the open.

"Evening, sir.'

'Well, Harrison?' Harrison was port watch, an A.B. with a paunch and an appetite to match. 'Anyone else with you?'

'Danny Allison's at the rear, sir.'

'Get him.' Carrick waited until the man returned with his shipmate. Hands clasped behind his back, he looked them over. 'Harrison, I spotted that cigarette a mile away.'

'Sorry, sir.' The A.B. shifted awkwardly. 'It's a cold night.'

'Then try moving around.' Carrick made it a bark. 'I'm taking a look inside. Both of you can make an additional patrol between here and the beach. Let me know when you get back – and no cigarettes.'

'Sir.' They saluted vigorously.

Carrick acknowledged, watched them set off, then tried the cottage door. It was still unlocked. He went in, closed and bolted it behind him, found the hall light switch, then quickly went through to the storeroom and opened the back door.

Arran slipped in and leaned back thankfully against the wall while he closed up again. She gave a sigh. 'Thanks.'

'We'll talk in the front room.' He led the way through and pulled the heavy curtains together before switching on the room light. 'Sit down, Arran.'

She settled herself on the rug by the hearth, where the fire still glowed a dull red. Shoes slipped off, slim legs tucked beneath her, she looked very much like a child, a badly frightened child. She was wearing a dark raincoat buckled over a heavy knit wool sweater and a russet brown tweed skirt, and the heavily mud-stained shoes beside her told their own story.

'Let me see your hands.'

Puzzled, she obeyed. Then, remembering the scar on her palm, she flushed. 'Making sure, Webb?'

'With your family it seems to pay.' He shoved his cap back on his head. 'Can you blame me?'

She turned towards the fire for a moment then shook her head. 'No. What's happened to my father?'

'Officially he's still held for questioning.' Carrick shrugged expressively. 'By tomorrow he'll probably have been charged. He told us about the money and his trips with John Page, but Dawe thinks he's still lying.'

'It's the truth!' She swung round, the protest strong in her voice. 'He needed the money for liquor one of the Irish boats was bringing over.'

'And he tried to tell us he could use scuba gear,' said Carrick pointedly. 'Only he tripped up when it came to detail.'

'The bank boat last night, you mean?' She cupped her face in her hands. 'Aline and I did that. I was the one who used the spear-gun, Webb – but I hit what I was aiming at. I usually do.'

'I'm glad,' he said with feeling. 'Why did you do it?'

'Because Dad and John were worried stiff when the *Thrift* was towed in here and they heard what had happened. We didn't know how much money had been stolen, but we did know their story wasn't likely to be believed – especially as they had seen the *Thrift* again on the Tuesday night while they were waiting for the Irishman.'

'Off the Abbey Isles?'

She nodded. 'They saw her, but she went past them.'

'Do you know the Irishman's name?'

'No.' She bit hard on her lip again. 'Webb, what about Aline and John? Why did they go, why didn't they come back again?' She sprang to her feet. 'They were here – I'll show you.'

He followed her to the kitchen. Three cups and saucers were set out on the table along with sugar and milk. Two cups still held dregs of tea, the third hadn't been used, and the teapot was still on the stove, half-full and long since cold.

'Why meet here?' he asked. 'Why not at the pier?'

'Because we were going to take the *Thrift's* daybook and the other papers with us to show Captain Shannon.'

He stared at her incredulously. 'They weren't burned?'

'No. He burned his passbook and told us to burn the rest. But – well, Aline and I decided against it. We kept them – they're hidden in the storeshed.'

'Then let's get them,' he said, gripping her hard by the shoulder. 'Arran, these books are his one chance now. That money is almost the only cash missing!' He saw hope come to life in the grey eyes, then followed her once more.

In the dry chill of the storeroom Arran MacKenna crossed straight over to the workbench, knelt down, and reached one hand into the narrow gap between bench and wall. She frowned, tried again, then looked up at Carrick in dismay.

'It's gone – but it was there, I swear it.'

Slowly Carrick nodded. 'I'll believe you, Arran. It makes pretty nasty sense. When Clapper Bell and I found that money somebody started shooting at us. He didn't score a hit – but maybe he wasn't trying, maybe the shooting was just for effect, because he already knew the *Thrift's* daybook had been taken from here.'

Still down on her knees, she stared up at him, bewildered. 'But why, Webb? What reason . . .?'

'Arran, I tried to tell you.' He helped her up and kept her hands in his. 'That book is at least part proof of your father's story. But while he and John Page are the main suspects – the only ones – somebody else can feel safe. Now listen, did anyone else know you had it?'

'No.' Her face had paled.

'Or about the money? Bob Tenford, for instance?'

She shook her head. 'We told nobody. And Aline and John – Webb, they aren't on the island. If they were I'd have found them.' Listlessly, she led the way back to the front room. 'Maybe if I went to Chief Inspector Dawe –'

'You'd land beside your father,' he told her bluntly. 'But don't blame Dawe. The way he sees it he'd have plain enough reason. Another thing, Arran – where does John get his money from? The police can't find an answer.'

'It's simple enough.' She looked at the dying peat fire and reached automatically for the brass scuttle beside it. 'When John sold out his vet practice down south part of the business was a plot of ground with boarding kennels. He sold it to a developer – for something like twenty thousand pounds.'

He watched as she lifted dried peat slabs one by one from the scuttle and placed them round the glowing embers. Next she took a fireside brush and shovel to sweep the ash scattered over the hearth's surround. Suddenly he gave a frown, dropped down beside her, and made her stop.

'What's wrong?' she demanded.

Gently, using the edge of one hand, he swept some of the ash and fragments together. 'This isn't from the fire, Arran. Look at it. Smell the bits that haven't burned.'

She obeyed, taking a pinch between finger and thumb and holding it to her nostrils. 'It – it's like tobacco, pipe tobacco. But John doesn't smoke a pipe. And Dad doesn't.'

'Somebody does – and knocked it out on the edge of the hearth. Got an envelope?' She fetched one, and he swept the fragments into it. 'Tenford smokes a pipe, Arran. If he crossed over from Buidhe and found John and Aline here wouldn't John tell him your plan?'

'He might.'

He nodded grimly. 'And Tenford has a small army at his back.'

'But he's John's friend . . .' Her eyes showed shock.

'Clapper Bell and I were going on a little trip to Buidhe tonight.' Carrick sealed the envelope and put it in his pocket. 'We'll be swimming. Where's the best place to get ashore unseen?'

She thought carefully. 'There's a patch of broken rock about a quarter mile north of the landing stage. It might do.'

'Fine. Now, about you. Have you a neighbour you can trust to keep you under cover?'

'Any of them would.'

He glanced at his watch. 'Then you'd better get going, by the storeshed way. These two characters will be on their way back by now.'

'I could come with you,' she protested.

'Not this trip.' He gave a quick grin of encouragement. 'Move – I'll see you later. And if Tenford has them – well, he'll be keeping them safe. Hostages are always handy when things are getting rough.'

She mustered an answering smile, nodded, and headed for the storeroom. Once she'd gone, he extinguished the cottage lights, went out by the front door, and stood there until the two shore patrol men returned.

'Nothing doing, sir,' reported Harrison glumly.

'It was worth a try.'

'Yessir.' Harrison glanced at his companion for support. 'Eh, any idea when we'll be off watch, sir?'

'Off watch?' Carrick raised an eyebrow at the enormity of the idea. 'You'll know when it happens. Stay here and keep your eyes open.'

Silent and far from happy, the two seamen watched him stride back towards the pier.

Chapter Six

Chief Petty Officer William 'Clapper' Bell surfaced from about two fathoms, looked around anxiously in the night darkness, and felt considerable relief at the sight of the other frogman bobbing in the rippling water a few yards away. He swam slowly across to where Carrick was floating and received a cheerful thumbs-up sign.

It was eight o'clock. Considering they'd crossed most of the distance between the harbour to Buidhe underwater and on a wrist-compass bearing, they'd done pretty well. Getting clear of *Marlin* unseen had been tricky, though Jumbo Wills had agreed to cover up their disappearance and had helped move their gear to a quiet corner by the cruiser's stern. But they'd made it – and now they were little more than a hundred yards off the island's shore, slap on target. The rocks Arran had described were almost dead ahead, a thin white line of surf breaking round their edges.

Carrick signalled again, they sank down from sight together, and then began finning forward. With the night guards on watch this was the only safe way to land on Buidhe – particularly if Carrick was right, if the few slender hunches and even more slender leads he'd strung together meant Tenford held the answers to so many things.

Carrick's legs brushed shingle. He stopped swimming, settled on the loose pebbles, then rose on his feet until his head broke surface. As the water cleared from his face-mask glass he took another careful look at the beach ahead before he started wading in towards the shore.

Once on dry land, their scuba lungs hidden under a mound of dry wrack weed beside a round, white-veined boulder, the two men rested briefly. Overhead, an occasional blink of pale moonlight broke through the ragged clouds to chase the shadows then let them reform in new menacing outline. A low wind rustled along the shore to merge with the murmur of the sea and somewhere back on Kenbeg a dog was barking – but otherwise all was silent

Dark, almost invisible shapes in their full-length rubber suits, the two men set off inland. Carrick led the way, setting a steady, cautious pace until at last he saw lights glinting through the trees ahead.

'That's the house, Clapper.' Carrick stopped for a moment, glad of the excuse. Out of its designed element, the rubber suit had all the qualities of a cumbersome sweat-bath. 'Having Doctor Perris as a dinner guest should mean Tenford's pretty well occupied. But keep your eyes open.'

Bell nodded and sucked his lips expectantly.

The storesheds behind the house were their first target. They reached them after a short, tense delay in the shelter of a wall while a guard went past. The man had a heavy pick-handle cradled under one arm and strolled along as if performing a dull, familiar routine.

Once he'd gone, they set to work – and drew a disappointment. None of the sheds were locked and their contents were either boxed bulbs or sacks of pungent chemical dressing. Carrick swore softly and looked towards the lights of the house, little more than a stone's throw away.

'How about tryin' there?' whispered Bell.

He shook his head. The greenhouses were next on his list.

They worked round to where the first of the big glass-walled blocks glinted in the moonlight. It was padlocked, but a few seconds' work with a short length of thin, tough brazing wire was enough to remove that obstacle. As the door edged open, a wave of dry heat from within stirred Carrick's memory – they'd found the cactus house. He left Bell as lookout and went in, the moonlight through the glass just sufficient to let him see his way. Once again, everything seemed peaceful and normal. They fixed the padlock back in position and moved on.

Two more greenhouses received the same attention and yielded exactly the same result.

'Do we bother wi' the rest?' asked Bell glumly. 'There's a hell o' a lot o' island, sir. Maybe we should roam around a bit more.'

Carrick had been asking himself the same question. It was after nine by his watch, which meant more than an hour had passed since they'd landed. He opened his mouth to answer then closed it again with a hiss of warning. They sank back into the shadows as the same guard moved past on his rounds, walking along a pathway between them and the house, heading in the direction of a bank of thick shrubbery.

'Let's take him on as guide,' breathed Carrick. 'If there's anything worth while around here he's bound to check it.'

Using what cover there was they began following. The man went through the shrubbery, turned north, then quickened his stride and kept on past a cluster of out-buildings. Farther on he stopped, swung a torchbeam ahead – and next moment seemed to disappear.

'Satan's gaiters!' Clapper Bell gaped incredulously.

The light glowed again, from below their eyeline, and Carrick relaxed. 'There's a fold in the ground, Clapper. Come on.'

They reached the edge of the dip and looked down. In the small hollow below sat yet another greenhouse, one bigger than the others they'd seen. The watchman was moving round it, his torch still shining.

'Ach.' Clapper Bell gave a snort, his crumpled face unimpressed. 'Another o' the things – no' much sense in bothering wi' it.'

Carrick pursed his lips. 'He didn't check the others. Maybe there's a reason.'

The man below finished his task and left the hollow again by a path running up the opposite slope. Once he'd gone, they went down and quickly located the block's centre door.

'Hey now, this is different!' Clapper Bell brightened as he saw the double set of patent locks. He tapped the glass and whistled. It was heavy-gauge, almost twice as solid as the usual horticultural variety.

'Now why – why for this one?' Carrick pressed his face against the glass, peering through. But the moonglow showed only an endless, motionless expanse of thin, tall-stemmed plants.

They worked slowly along the side of the block until they found a row of windows set just above chest level. The windows were tightly shut – all except one with a tiny quarter-inch gap between part of its frame and the surrounding cross-pieces, a mere warping of ill-fitting material. It was enough to let the brazing wire slide through.

A spell of delicate probing, and Clapper Bell had the wire hooked round the inner handle, easing it back. A light pull, and the window swung open.

'My turn.' Carrick nodded, gripped the sill, put his left foot into Bell's cupped hands, and heaved himself up. Perched on the sill, he listened for a moment to the low hum of the block's heating plant and sniffed the heavy warm-damp odour of the plants.

'Page?' He kept his voice low. All remained silent. He took a deep breath, swung one leg over the sill into the building – then froze where he was as a high-pitched alarm bell began a noisy, angry clamour.

'That's done it!' Clapper Bell tugged urgently at his other leg. 'Pack it in, quick!'

'Hold on – we'll take something, anyway.' Carrick grabbed a leaf from the nearest plant, tore it loose, then jumped down, hitting the ground on hands and knees. The alarm bell still clamouring, they scrambled back up the slope and out of the dip. Torchbeams were already starting to head their way from the direction of the house.

'Head for the beach,' said Carrick bitterly. 'It's either that or fight a war.'

They started off, moving as fast as the suits would allow, travelling a straight-line course across a patchwork of tilled plots and shallow ditches.

'What the hell happened anyway?' panted Clapper Bell. 'Some kind o' alarm wire?'

'Or a guard beam.' Carrick stuffed the plant leaf inside a pocket as they hurried on.

'And why the green stuff?' demanded Bell breathlessly. 'Do you – do you need a souvenir?'

'Maybe.' Carrick had his eye on the thick, dark line of bushes on ahead. As they reached it a sudden massive shove in the back sent him sprawling. Next moment Bell dropped beside him, pointing ahead. Someone was coming straight towards them, crashing through the bushes in his haste to answer the alarm summons.

The greenhouse bell stopped its clamour – and the guard coming through the bushes stumbled into sight a moment later, breathing heavily, the heavy pick-shaft in his right hand held high and ready. He saw Clapper Bell a fraction of a second before that black, spectre-like figure catapulted up from the ground. They went down together, and the man managed one stifled yelp before Bell hit him twice – fast, chopping blows with the edge of the hand on the side of his neck.

He went limp. They picked him up, dragged him along the edge of the bushes to a drainage ditch, and dumped him in, out of sight.

Carrick turned, then groaned aloud. The torches from the house were coming closer, the men behind them shouting as they came – coming from the north strung out in a long line and travelling fast, other torchlights were now hurrying towards them. Roused from their bunkhouse, the island's main labour force was arriving on the scene.

They were caught in a squeeze.

He stood where he was, conscious of Bell eyeing him, waiting for a lead. Fight or run, the bo'sun would take it as an order.

'If we separate we might have more of a chance. A straight break for –' Carrick stopped, bewildered. A vivid flash of light had flared from the south, beyond the house, a light followed by a flat, growling blast and a sudden flicker of flames licking high into the air.

'Where's that comin' from?' demanded Clapper Bell, startled.

'The boathouse, or the boats at the landing stage.' Carrick grabbed him by the arm in a new breath of hope. 'Head for those bushes and make like a mole.'

He took a last swift glance around as they reached the dark mass of shrubbery. Already the men coming from the house were reacting as he'd hoped. Their torches were flickering back along the route towards the landing stage, their shouts were beginning to grow distant. He mouthed a silent prayer and dived into the bushes, burrowing down into the thick leafy growth, cursing the diving suit again for its awkwardness yet knowing he'd one more cause to bless its dull black finish. Somewhere near, twigs crackled as Clapper Bell wriggled into hiding – and then they lay still, waiting.

Soon the first of the men from the bunkhouse came crashing past. One forced his way through the bushes near enough for Carrick to glimpse the heavy boots and trousered legs – then the whole pack swept past and were gone. The flames to the south now formed a red glow in the sky.

128

'Whoever started that wee bonfire got us off the hook, that's for sure,' rumbled Clapper Bell, wincing as he eased his cramped muscles and cautiously followed Carrick out into the open.

'And I've an idea who,' said Carrick softly. 'We've stirred up enough trouble, Clapper. Time to go.'

They travelled steadily, crossed a last thin straggle of tall grass, and saw the white line of the shore ahead. The moon glinted on the sea beyond, and the coastline was familiar. They were on the fringe of the rocky stretch where they'd landed.

'Damn nice t' be back,' said Clapper Bell happily.

Carrick nodded. 'Our gear's fairly close – but take it easy.'

They moved carefully over the jagged outcrops until they spotted the rounder boulder with the patch of weed at its base. Clapper Bell made a noise like a purr and stepped forward ... then stayed where he was as a firm, metallic click echoed near at hand.

'Webb?' Low-pitched but fairly confident, the voice came from only yards away.

Carrick gave a grin of relief. 'Come on out, Arran.'

She stepped into view, the green cold-water diving suit fitting her figure like a glove, a cocked spear-gun cradled under one arm, a lightweight single-cylinder aqualung strapped to her back.

For once Clapper Bell could only splutter, lost for words.

Carrick looked back along the beach. The glow by the landing stage was beginning to die down. 'All your own work?'

She gave a brief, impatient nod. 'Yes – Webb, what about Aline and John? Did you –'

'No.' He shrugged his regret and knew it inadequate. 'We landed smack in trouble when we were still just prying around.'

'I see.' She stood biting her lip for an instant. 'We'd better not stay here.'

Carrick nodded. By his side, Clapper Bell was already dragging the two scuba sets from under the weed. 'What about you, Arran? How did you find this spot?'

It was her turn to shrug. 'I watched you leave *Marlin* and tried to follow, but I lost you on the way across. I knew you were landing somewhere on this stretch, so I just kept on looking until I found your scubas.'

'And the fire?' He began buckling on his harness.

'I was down near the landing stage when the alarm bell began. The watchman there started running – like everyone else, I suppose. There were some cans of boat fuel lying around, and I thought it might help.' She spoke in matter-of-fact style, as if discussing a knitting pattern or a cook-book recipe. 'So I set the boatshed on fire then cut loose one of the boats and pulled it out into the channel until it began drifting. It'll maybe give them the idea that was how you got away. Then ... well, I came back here.'

'Where will you go now?' He fastened the weight-belt round his waist and was ready.

'The *Gooshgash*. It's been searched, it's practically under *Marlin's* nose – it should be safe enough.'

'About Aline and John –'

She shook her head. 'Don't say it. I know you tried.'

'We won't leave it at this,' he promised. 'We'll have to go carefully, for their sake, but –'

Clapper Bell cut him short. 'People comin',' he said softly. 'The natives are no' very friendly round here, remember?'

They pulled down their face-masks, waded out into the sea, and began swimming.

Captain Shannon had a calm, almost bored expression on his face. He was in his cabin, settled comfortably in an armchair. A glass of whisky was on the table by his side, a copy of the current Admiralty list of Notices to Mariners

130

lay on his lap and there were carpet slippers on his feet. He heard a soft knock on the cabin door and glanced at his watch. It was a few minutes before midnight.

'Come in.'

He gave a faint, frosty smile as the cabin door opened and Carrick entered. He inspected his Chief Officer's uniform with some care, then nodded. 'Close the door, mister.' As Carrick obeyed, he cleared his throat with delicate care. 'Heard the news, eh?'

'Sir?' Carrick stood very still, waiting.

'No, maybe not.' Shannon tossed the Notices to Mariners on the floor. 'You've been with the bo'sun, I'm told. Off on a hike to have another look at MacKenna's oyster farm, according to the second mate. Pity.' He rose to his feet and crossed over to the corner cupboard. 'If you'd been over here you'd have heard the excitement. Doctor Perris brought the story back from Buidhe about an hour ago. Seems they had prowlers over there – two at least, they reckon. A watchman was clubbed, a dinghy was stolen and Tenford's boatshed was burned down.'

'Any idea where they came from or what they wanted, sir?'

'Nope.' Shannon made a strange noise in his throat then opened the cupboard, standing with his back towards Carrick. 'Doctor Perris says Tenford thinks they were locals from Kenbeg, our Chief Inspector's theory is that it might have been Page and the MacKenna girls, especially when they took this boat. As for how they got out to Buidhe in the first instance, Tenford's theory appears to be that they waded across the shallows at the north end – even though his watchman there swears nobody passed him.'

'What's your theory, sir?'

'Mine? I wasn't there.' Shannon turned, his short, dark beard twitching with a dry amusement. The cabin light gleamed on the filled glass in his hand. 'Have a drink, mister. It's a cold night to have been out for a – a walk.'

131

'That's how I found it, sir.' Carrick returned the captain's grin, took the glass, and sipped the whisky.

'Now sit down,' said Shannon, a grimmer note in his voice. 'You'd better know this first. Sawny MacKenna asked to see me tonight. He's worried stiff about those girls, worried enough to have stopped being stubborn. He gave me the name of the Irishman who was shipping him the booze, and we've radioed the Irish authorities asking them to check.'

Carrick gave a soft whistle. 'That should make a difference.'

'If it's true, enough to make Dawe not nearly so happy about things. He's worried already.' Shannon perched himself on the edge of his chair and took a long swallow from his glass. 'Now it's your turn, mister. Let's have it – the lot. I've time to listen.' His mouth tightened. 'Plenty of time, and plenty of interest.'

Carrick nodded. 'The way things are, I was coming to see you anyway.'

He talked and Shannon listened, asking only an occasional question, the rest of the whisky lying forgotten in its glass. At last, Shannon gave a long sigh and rose to his feet.

'Tenford ... well, why not? And this greenhouse interests me. Double locks, heavy glass, alarm bells ... all that for a bunch of potted plants?'

'That's all I could see,' admitted Carrick.

Shannon sniffed testily. 'All anybody was meant to see, if they got near it. Use your head, man. Even ruddy orchids don't merit that kind of protection.' He paused at the thought. 'They weren't orchids, were they?'

'I don't know, but I got this.' Carrick took his warrant card from the inside pocket of his jacket, opened it, and handed Shannon the torn plant leaf he'd placed there a short time before. It was small, dark green in colour, its five palm-like lobes serrated along their edges.

'Hmm.' Shannon frowned down at it. 'Well, no sense asking me. I'm no gardener, and it could be a new kind of carrot for all I know.' He bunched one fist and slapped it impatiently against his other hand. 'But what the hell are we up against? Smuggling? That's small-time stuff in the main. Security stuff? There's the rocket test range in the north, but –' He shook his head. 'No, that hardly makes sense. Anyway, what I suppose should be worrying us now is what's happened to Page and the MacKenna girl.'

'If he's got them, sir – we can't be sure,' qualified Carrick unwillingly.

'If . . . if . . . I know.' Shannon's face darkened. 'If he has them, and if he was behind what happened on the *Thrift* –' He left the rest unsaid. 'Right. I'll put a man to watch that catamaran. If anyone shows near it he'll report to me personally. After that I'm going to have a long talk with our detective friend.'

'Want me along, sir?'

'You?' Shannon considered, then shook his head. 'No, you get some sleep, mister. I still want you to work the *Thrift* across to Mallaig in the morning. Take this piece of greenery and the pipe tobacco ash with you – I'll arrange the rest.' He saw the look on Carrick's face and gave a growl. 'Don't try to argue, mister. Tenford's drifter is laid on as your escort. One way or another, tonight's little episode should have him rattled, even if he thinks it may have been Arran MacKenna and some of her father's pals. He'll be worried. This trip to the mainland might be very handy from his point of view. Understand?'

'I'll keep my eyes open,' said Carrick, seeing the strength of the argument.

'Do that,' said Shannon softly. 'If anything happens, you may only get the one chance. Remember that.'

The wardroom steward shook Carrick awake at 6 a.m. and laid a steaming mug of tea on the table beside his bunk.

'There's a bit o' mist around, but it's not too bad a morning, sir,' reported the man cheerfully. He reached into the top pocket of his white mess-coat and produced an envelope. 'Captain asked me to give you this with his compliments – told me to say, he's had a late night and doesn't want to be wakened.'

'Thanks.' Carrick took the envelope and yawned himself awake as the man went out. Then he took a gulp of the strong, scalding liquid before opening the message. Shannon's precise copperplate handwriting ran to one sentence:

I have come to an understanding with Dawe, who will co-operate for the time being.

It was, decided Carrick, a masterpiece of understatement against the background of what must have passed between the two men. He tasted the tea again then, as its warmth percolated through him, he swung his legs over the side of the bunk, found and lit a cigarette, and began dressing.

By six-thirty he had eaten a solitary breakfast in his cabin and was ready. A quiet throb of engines reached his ears as he went on deck, glancing around in the grey dawn light. Astern, the catamaran's squat twin-hulled shape was still tied alongside the pier. His face softened for a moment as he thought of the girl probably still asleep aboard her. His eyes caught a slight movement just inside the companionway door by *Marlin's* stern and he gave a flickering grin, remembering Shannon's words. Arran could sleep soundly.

He crossed the deck to the seaward side. The white hull of the *Thrift* was already lying alongside the fishery cruiser with two of *Marlin's* ratings aboard and her engine ticking over.

'Mr Carrick.' The thin nervous voice made him turn. Henry Campbell stood behind him, pale and shivering, a bulging briefcase in one hand, his thin frame wrapped in a heavy coat, a scarf wound round his neck.

134

'All set?' asked Carrick cheerfully.

The bank investigator nodded with a grim resolution. 'I suppose so. How . . . how long will this crossing take? I . . . well, I'll admit to a certain distrust of sea travel.'

'No need to worry about it,' soothed Carrick. 'From here to Mallaig is about fifty miles, but the sea should be calm enough. We can probably coax ten knots out of the *Thrift*, so about five hours should do it.'

'Five –' Campbell closed his eyes at the thought.

'The sooner we're started the sooner we're there.' Carrick watched with a tinge of malicious amusement as the man climbed awkwardly over the side and was helped aboard the bank boat. Out in the bay, Tenford's drifter had already cast off her mooring and was nosing slowly towards them. He took a last look towards the catamaran, then turned for the rail.

From Kenbeg, their course lay south-east in an almost straight line across the empty width of sea which stretched between the Hebridean chain and the scatter of inner islands which fringed the mainland. The *Thrift* led the way, travelling steadily, her engine running smoothly. Tenford's drifter, half as large again as the bank boat, kept a steady station some five hundred yards astern, her helmsman showing no inclination to close the gap.

Soon the sun came up, to help the light wind vanquish the last wisps of mist. The sea was calm enough to encourage even Campbell to muster an interest in his surroundings and come up from below to stand in the cockpit. Carrick rummaged through the boat's signal locker, found a spare Central Bank pennant, and had it run up on the broken stub of the mast. It flapped lazily, complementing the Red Ensign at her stern – and Campbell squared his shoulders a little at the sight, as if it was a symbol that he might survive the experience.

135

More than once, Carrick turned his glasses on the drifter astern – and one of the two ratings beside him was under orders to keep a constant eye on their trailing escort. Carrick counted two men in her wheelhouse and another pair who seemed to spend most of their time lounging by her for'ard hatch. The next time he looked, one of the men in the wheelhouse had vanished and each time thereafter the count was three. But if the men concerned were aware of his inspection they gave no sign.

The *Thrift* throbbed on through the morning, changing course a little to keep the growing bulk of the islands of Canna and Rhum to starboard while the tall black mountains of Skye, a few capped with snow, soon formed her horizon to the north. A low, greasy swell began running as the islands closed in, enough to send Campbell back below. But Carrick, watching the sky, felt reassured – if there was to be any break for the worse in the weather there was still no sign. The inevitable tea was brewed, the bank boat's engines ran without a falter, and he waved a greeting as one of the big red-and-black MacBrayne steamers swept majestically past, outward bound for Stornoway and the isles.

They reached Mallaig a little before noon. Fishing harbour and steamer port, railhead and market-place, the terminal point of the Road to the Isles, a hub of communication, it was still only a village of some six hundred souls – and few if any of them seemed to be paying the slightest attention as the *Thrift* came in round the harbour point.

'Drifter's dropping back, sir,' sang one of the seamen suddenly.

Carrick glanced round from the helm. The gap had widened, from its previous five hundred to close on a thousand yards, but she was still coming on.

'Keep an eye on her.' There was little more he could do. An open launch was chugging its way out of the harbour and running on a course close to his own, and he was

136

already starting to throttle back to head the *Thrift* in towards the railway pier. The launch passed close, a man crouching over her engine – then a flurry of hand-signals from the pierhead began guiding them round to a vacant berth.

'Drifter's out of sight, sir,' reported the seaman. 'The pier's between us.'

Carrick swore to himself as he edged the bank boat alongside the pier and saw her safely moored fore and aft. Henry Campbell appeared from below as her fenders bumped lightly against the pier's timbers. White-faced but happy, the man moved eagerly towards the waiting ladder. Carrick let him go up first then followed. A uniformed police inspector and a sergeant were standing at the top, accompanied by a couple of harbour officials.

He ignored them for a moment, looking back across the water. Then he relaxed with a sigh. The drifter was coming in, moving at little more than a crawl, heading towards another berth further up the harbour.

'No trouble on the trip, Webb?' The police inspector, a tall, ruddy-faced man, young for his rank, had stepped beside him.

'Hello, Pete.' Carrick gave an apologetic grin. Peter Muir was an old acquaintance, just as Mallaig was a regular port of call in the Fishery Protection schedule.

'If it's the drifter, leave it to us,' said Muir softly. 'She's going to her usual berth and I've a man over there.'

'Fine.' Carrick gave a quick nod of understanding then crossed to where Henry Campbell was standing.

'That's it, Mr Campbell – wasn't too bad, was it?'

The bank investigator took a deep breath. 'It could have been worse,' he admitted. 'But now that I'm here I'll need to telephone Head Office right away.'

Inspector Muir guided him towards the harbour officials. 'They'll fix that for you – and anything else you need. Oh, and I'll have a couple of men on guard at the *Thrift*. She'll be safe enough.'

Campbell nodded and trotted on his way.

'Well, now he's out of our hair –' Muir turned back to Carrick and gave him a long, quizzical look. 'I've had a string of instructions about you from Headquarters, Webb. "Put yourself at the disposal of Chief Officer Carrick within reasonable limits" was the phrase they used.' He grimaced. 'Trouble is, nobody ever says what "reasonable limits" means. I'd say you've been ruffling somebody's feathers – like a certain C.I.D. man I know, would that be it?'

'It makes a start,' admitted Carrick.

'And I've a package to collect,' reminded Muir. 'We've a couple of Scientific Branch characters waiting on it – they arrived about an hour ago.'

Carrick produced the thick envelope in which he'd brought both the tobacco fragments and the plant leaf. Muir beckoned his sergeant, handed it over, and sent the man on his way.

'How long till you go back out?' he queried. 'I've six men detailed to go with you for special duty on Kenbeg.'

'That's up to Tenford's men on the drifter,' Carrick told him, glancing at his watch. 'It's twelve-fifteen now – I'd reckon they should be ready by one o'clock. Like to walk round with me and find out?'

'Aye.' Muir gave a fractional wink. 'Let's say it would do no harm for us to look them over.'

They took their time walking through the bustle of dockside activity, past a line of fishing boats queuing to load ice for their holds from waiting lorries then threading through a maze of cargo which dockers were unloading from a coaster. Two grey-hulled naval auxiliary craft and a larger lighthouse tender lying farther out in the midst of a cluster of smaller boats and yachts – for its size, Mallaig harbour had plenty of custom.

The drifter, when they reached it, was tied next to a rust-hulled collier. Two of her crew were on deck working a block and tackle from her foremast boom to lower a bulky

packing case aboard. Other packing cases lay on the quay-
side, being unloaded from a canvas-topped van by another
pair of men.

'Where's the skipper?' asked Carrick as he reached
them.

One of the men, thick-set, wearing the inevitable jersey
and seaboots, lowered the packing case he was manoeuvring and straightened up, wiping sweat from his brow.

'That's me – the name's O'Neil.' He stuck a cigarette in
his mouth and lit it, eyeing Carrick and the policeman over
the flame of his lighter. 'Well, everything okay? You didn't
seem t' need any help on the way over.'

'We'd no problems,' said Carrick evenly. 'What time will
you be ready to leave?'

The drifter skipper shrugged. 'I've this stuff t' load first
– an' then I've promised the boys a beer or two.'

Carrick glanced at the second man, leaning back against
the van's cab. 'Nobody told me you'd be picking up
cargo.'

'Don't blame him,' grinned O'Neil. 'He's just the driver.
Mr Tenford doesn't believe in wasting trips. This is some
machinery spares we hadn't room t' take when we were
over yesterday. The boss radioed that we'd collect today.'

Inspector Muir wandered past and examined the cases
with a casual interest. They were stencilled with the name
of a Glasgow engineering firm, and the way the men had
been handling them showed they were no light weight.

'All right,' nodded Carrick. 'But the sooner we're on our
way the better I'll like it.'

'Give us another hour,' said O'Neil easily. 'When will
those cops we're taking over show up?'

'In plenty of time,' grunted Inspector Muir. 'So leave
some room for them.'

'She's no royal yacht, but we'll try.' The drifter skipper
gave a cynical salute and turned his back on them. The
boat's lifting tackle began clattering again; and they
walked away.

'Not much of a welcome, laddie,' said Muir dryly. 'I could have told you about the cargo – I've asked Headquarters to get details from the makers.'

'Could we check with your lookout?' Carrick pursed his lips. 'We saw only three crewmen, Pete. I'm pretty certain there were four aboard her.'

'Right now – but the term's "plain clothes man on observation duty."' Muir guided him round a stack of baled wool shipped in from one of the islands and across to a small wooden hut. Above its door was the faded sign: FISH BUYERS AGENCY.

They went in. Behind the small counter which ran across its width a man sat at a desk. He looked up, nodded, and bent his head back to the account book he was studying.

'We wait here.' Muir took out his cigarettes, offered one to Carrick, and they shared a match. In a few seconds the door opened again, and a young man in overalls and a nondescript muffler came in.

'Well?' queried Muir.

'Nothing unloaded and nobody gone ashore here, sir,' reported the plain clothes constable briefly. Then he hesitated. 'But I'm not so sure about what happened just before she came in.'

'Eh?' Muir's brow wrinkled in a sudden frown. 'What do you mean?'

'Outside the harbour, sir. There was an open launch going out –'

Carrick nodded, feeling a grey foreboding gathering within him. 'One man aboard. We passed her.'

'That's the one,' agreed the constable swiftly. 'She's not local, though she's been seen around before.'

'Never mind that,' snapped Muir. 'What happened?'

'Well –' The constable eyed him warily. 'I couldn't get a clear view, because I was waiting over here for the drifter coming in. But the launch was heading out for her, and then it went out of sight, close in on the drifter's seaward side. The drifter seemed to have stopped. Next thing I saw was the drifter heading in here and the launch starting to steer south, along the coast.'

'Damn and to hell!' Muir gave a groan. 'Why didn't you report this right away?'

'It would have meant leaving the dockside uncovered,' said the constable defensively. 'Then I saw you coming this way –'

Muir grunted acceptance. 'Right. If the launch headed south that probably means a landing farther down – and the main Inverness road follows the coast.' He rubbed a hand across his chin. 'You're supposed to go back on that drifter, Webb.'

Carrick shook his head. 'Put my men aboard along with your police detail and tell her skipper I've had fresh orders – that I've to stay with the *Thrift*.'

'Sounds reasonable.' Muir glared briefly at his constable. 'Get hold of Sergeant Finlay. Tell him what we're doing.'

Chapter Seven

A slim black M.G. hardtop, the county car had been left parked close to the harbourmaster's office. Muir slid behind the wheel, threw open the other door, and had the car started and moving before Carrick was fully settled in the passenger seat.

Driving with an intense, angry concentration, the policeman had them clear of Mallaig in record time. As the road widened his foot rammed harder on the accelerator and the car leapt forward, the needle pointers on the rev. counter and speedometer sweeping upwards. Carrick clung to the dashboard grab handle as they swung round a corner in a brief scream of tyre rubber.

'I'm taking a chance,' growled Muir, his eyes fixed ahead. 'If I wanted to land something in broad daylight in this part of the world then I'd try for Balbeg. It's an old ferry point, about ten miles down the coast. Used to belong to a retired fisherman who'd sail you across to the islands if the price was right – but he drowned when I was a kid and the place hasn't been used since.'

Carrick nodded while they flashed past a slow-moving tractor and trailer. Ahead, the road wound on, keeping roughly parallel with the coastline, sometimes running alongside the railway track which followed the same general route, skirting the fringe of the hills beyond, hills which rapidly gave way to high, sombre mountains. Up there, in a desolation of green moss and purple heather, lay an empty world where a man might wander for a week and never find a trace of human habitation. If the launch reached its destination and whoever was aboard had the chance to strike into that desolation –

They kept at the same relentless pace, the M.G.'s horn blasting a strident warning as it streaked through the occasional handful of houses bordering the road, handfuls which earned the name of townships on an otherwise empty map. At last, as the road came back to the coast again after a brief curve inland, Carrick saw what he had been praying for moving on the grey-blue water ahead – an open launch, about a half mile off shore and heading south.

'Pete –'

Muir took time for a quick glance and gave a soft murmur of triumph. 'We've got 'em, laddie. Got 'em, with just enough margin to set up for a kill.'

'How far to go?' The car's speed was already overtaking the boat. Straining his eyes, bracing himself against the swaying motion, Carrick could make out two figures sitting near the stern.

'About a couple of miles.' Muir was happier now, but the speedometer stayed steady. 'There's a shingle beach and the remains of a landing stage. Up above there's a couple of old cottages, both derelict. In summer there's often the odd holiday tent pitched beside them – kids up from the city. But not this late in the year.'

Another bend in the road hid the launch from view and when it reappeared it was far behind them. Soon the route swung inland again, and seconds later Muir knocked the M.G.'s stubby gear lever into neutral, took his foot off the accelerator, and let the car coast to a halt beside a patch of thick whin bushes.

'Out,' he said briefly. 'We'd better hike the rest. They may have a reception committee waiting.'

They left the car and began walking, cutting across the rough wasteland towards the shore, then climbing a short, steep rise. At the top, they looked down on a tiny semi-circle of pebbled beach with a dilapidated black skeleton of a landing stage poking out into the water, its final stretch reduced to a few wooden piles standing like decayed, forgotten teeth. A tall grey heron stalked a stiff, majestic path along the weed at its base.

Wordlessly, Muir nudged him and thumbed to the right. The two ruined cottages sat side by side – and a dark grey delivery truck was parked between them, its chrome glittering in the pale sunlight.

'No sign of anyone,' mused Carrick.

Muir nodded. 'Let's take a wee look, eh?'

They went down. The cottages were empty and the truck's radiator was barely lukewarm. At its rear doors the narrow track of bicycle tyres showed clear on the sandy soil, snaking along the rough path towards the main road.

'Brought the truck here, then pedalled in to collect the launch.' Muir rubbed his hands gently together. 'Well, it should be here soon.'

Carrick crossed back to the nearest of the cottages and stopped at the gaping hole which had once been its doorway. 'In here, Pete – let them come to us.'

It was a suggestion after Muir's heart. They went in, brushed past the last few shreds of peeling wallpaper and crumbled lathing, and settled down to wait. Soon the slow throb of an engine reached their ears and the launch came into view, heading round a small foreland then nosing in towards the landing stage. As it drew nearer, one of the two men aboard moved up to the bow. The launch engine died, and, as it drifted alongside the plank walkway, the man at the bow jumped out. He twisted a mooring rope round one of the uprights then hurried ashore and began crunching over the shingle towards them.

'Heads down,' murmured Muir. They pulled farther back, out of sight, while the footsteps came closer, stopped, then continued. They heard the rear doors of the truck squeak open then slam shut again and at last, whistling,

144

the man began walking back. Carrick inched forward and peered round the edge of the doorway. The long dark hair and slouching gait were ample identification of the new arrival.

'Tommy Vanden, one of Tenford's night guards,' he said softly. 'He "co-operated" with us just enough to put the finger on MacKenna and Page.'

'Fine – and a wee change from chasing kids for football in the street.' Muir grinned, slid a short ebony-black baton from its tunic pocket, wrapped the leather thong of the handle round his wrist, then found his own viewpoint.

Vanden was back at the launch. He spoke to the other man, a thin laugh rang out, and they set to work. A filled and bulky sack was dragged out of the launch, dumped for a moment on the boards of the landing stage then, one at each end, the two men began carrying it ashore.

Muir sucked hard on his teeth. 'Well?'

Carrick drew him back from the doorway. 'We'll jump them at the truck. I'll take Vanden.'

The slow, heavy footsteps came gradually nearer. One of the men was breathing heavily, cursing at the weight of their burden. The footsteps stopped, the rear doors of the truck squeaked again, and Carrick drew a deep breath.

'Now, Pete!'

They sprang from the doorway as the men from the launch spun round. Vanden was standing beside the sack. His companion, a squat, heavily built stranger with a round, sallow face, had been in the act of securing the opened doors.

Vanden recovered first. As Carrick's initial rush slammed him back against the side of the truck the man still managed to block a hard blow aimed at his head and counter with a wild jab to Carrick's jaw. Carrick rode the blow, had a brief glimpse of Muir already rolling on the ground with the other man, then had his hands too full to pay further attention.

Fighting with a frantic desperation, Vanden broke free and staggered back along the side of the truck. His hand dived into the hip pocket of his denims, there was a clack of levered steel, and the six-inch blade of a flick-knife glinted in his right fist.

The blade raked up. Carrick dodged it with a muscle-wrenching twist of his body, gripped the knife-wrist with his left hand, and hammered his right fist into Vanden's mouth. Before Vanden could recover, he tripped him with a fast leg-movement and they fell together, hitting the ground beside the front wheels of the truck.

'This . . . time.' Vanden grunted as he strained. Veins corded on his forehead as he tried to force the knife-point towards Carrick's throat.

Carrick took a gambling change of tactics. He let the knife come down a fraction then made his own effort, summoning every ounce of energy he possessed into a massive leverage. The knife-arm hinged back – and as it did, he butted his head hard into Vanden's twisted face. The man sucked breath in a whistle of pain and Carrick seized his chance to shift both hands to the knife-wrist. He heaved – and the knife-arm swung back, Vanden's elbow hitting the metal of the wheel's hub-cap with a clattering, piston-like force. The man screamed and the knife fell from his hand. But he still swung his knee up in a vicious in-fighting jab, connecting hard with Carrick's stomach.

A sick haze of agony shot through Carrick's body. Working on sheer animal reflex, he grabbed Vanden by his long, oily hair and smashed his head twice in succession against the truck's wheel before he let go. Vanden tried to rise to his feet, buckled at the knees, then pitched forward and began to crawl away in blind, aimless terror.

Teeth clenched, Carrick forced himself upright, staggered after the man, and once again gripped him by the hair, pulling his head back.

'No . . .' The word came as a moan from Vanden's battered mouth.

Carrick nodded, his lips a thin white line against the weather-beaten tan of his face. He stood where he was, swaying slightly, breathing heavily, the pain gradually receding. He looked round and saw Muir. One lapel of the policeman's tunic had been ripped loose and he was busy straightening the crumpled remains of his tie. But his thick-set opponent was lying face-down at his feet.

'Ach, I'm out of training,' admitted Muir. 'I had to thump this lard-bladder a couple of times with my stick before he'd quieten.' He raised an inquiring eyebrow. 'You all right?'

Carrick rubbed one hand hard and several times across the back of his neck, took another deep breath, and nodded.

'Good.' Muir crossed over, looked down at Vanden with a mild interest, then twitched a set of handcuffs from his pocket. 'Let's fix them up, Webb. I haven't seen mine before, but I've a feeling Records will know him.'

They dragged Vanden across to where the other man lay, handcuffed them wrist to wrist, then turned towards the sack. Its top was sewn shut with a length of tough sailcord. Carrick laid one hand on the coarse weave, felt the shape beneath, then stared up at his companion, his mouth suddenly kiln-dry.

'Pete –'

Muir understood. He turned, grabbed the fallen flick-knife from the ground, and began slashing at the sailcord. Carrick winced as it opened and he saw the close-cropped fair hair of the man within. They pulled him clear. John Page was pale and limp, his eyes were closed, and his wrists had been roped to his ankles. They slashed the ropes, straightened him out, then Carrick pressed an ear against the young vet's chest.

'Is he . . .' Muir waited anxiously.

At last Carrick looked up, his face showing a degree of relief.

147

'There's still a heartbeat.' He bent down again, his fingers easing back Page's right eyelid. The eye stared up, blank and unmoving, the pupil contracted to little more than a pinhead.

'Narcotic trauma.' Muir swore quietly but with a depth of feeling. 'Webb, you said there was a girl –'

They hurried down to the launch. The second sack was lying beneath the centre thwart, its fabric soaked on the underside where slack water had swirled against it from the bilges. The knife cut it open.

Aline MacKenna had been treated in the same style. Gently, angrily, they carried her up the beach and laid her beside Page.

Muir stood back and looked down at them in a mixture of fury and bewilderment. 'What the hell kind of devilry is worth this?'

'I wish I knew, Pete,' said Carrick wearily. 'But they're alive – you could say they're lucky.'

The next half-hour passed quickly. Once Muir had radioed from the M.G. for an ambulance and a patrol van they made Aline MacKenna and Page as comfortable as they could then turned to their prisoners.

Tommy Vanden, bruised and sullen, invited them to go to hell before he closed his mouth like a steel trap. His fat-faced comrade had a driving licence which gave his name as Joseph Lucan with a home address in Manchester. An old bucket lay handy beside the cottages, and Carrick half-filled it with sea water then threw it on the man's face to bring him round. Lucan spluttered back to life and swore pungently as he discovered the handcuff round his wrist.

'Quieten down,' snapped Carrick. 'You're in enough trouble already, Lucan. Where were you taking Page and the girl?'

'To a holiday camp – where else?' Lucan's expression was far from pretty.

'Leave them,' shrugged Muir. 'They'll be a deal more polite once I've got them in a cell. And I'll check the truck out with Motor Taxation.'

Carrick nodded. It might help – if the plates were genuine, if the truck wasn't on the stolen list, if its details didn't trace back to some accommodation address. But it was necessary routine, the kind of routine which sometimes paid off.

Ambulance and patrol van arrived together. He helped the ambulance crew move their two patients aboard by stretcher, saw Muir busy detailing his men between the moored launch, the truck and the prisoners, and gave him a brief wave before he climbed into the ambulance. Its doors closed, the engine fired, and they set off.

Mallaig's cottage hospital was small but well equipped and the doctor who met them was middle-aged, with an unlit stump of cheroot between his teeth and a heavy tweed suit beneath his crumpled white coat.

A nurse hovering at his side, he set to work without a word. Respiration, pulse, heart, temperature, eyes . . . he padded a deliberate, unhurried way between Page and the girl.

At last, a thoughtful frown on his face, he beckoned Carrick over. 'Hypodermic administration of a morphine derivative – at least, that's what I'd say at an educated guess. Know anything that might confirm it?'

'Nothing, sorry.' Carrick shook his head. Aline's breathing was shallow and laboured, and, like Page, her face looked pale and cold yet was covered by a film of perspiration. 'I wish I did, Doctor –'

'Hodson's the name. And I'm no expert in this – I've been cramming up on textbooks since I was told to stand by.' He gnawed on the cheroot stump. 'All right, we'll see if we can tickle them round a bit. Nurse –' He turned to the nurse and gave a quick, low-voiced instruction. She

149

hurried off and returned within seconds carrying an instrument tray.

'Not so long ago about all we could have done would be to start stomach-washing and keep them warm,' said Doctor Hodson conversationally, setting to work. 'Now we've got this stuff –' he held up a small, sealed bottle and checked its label – 'stuff that's a specific antidote. Nalorphine, doses ten to forty milligrammes, and has to be handled with care or it could foul up the existing respiratory depression.' Deftly he drew the required dose into a hypodermic, squirted a little from the needle's tip, then turned towards Page. 'We'll try him, for a start. You'll find it interesting – like the old magic wand routine, if we're on the right track.'

'And if you're not?'

'No harm done.' The nurse had already cut open Page's shirt sleeve and had swabbed an area of skin with surgical spirit. Doctor Hodson's lips drew back from clenched teeth as he selected his spot, pushed home the needle and depressed the syringe. 'First time . . . not bad for an intravenous, eh, nurse?' He drew the needle clear, rubbed the puncture mark with his thumb, then took Page's wrist in his hand, feeling for the pulse.

For a long minute nothing happened, the silence in the room broken only by Aline MacKenna's slow, laboured breathing and the steady tick of the heavy fob watch which the nurse wore pinned to her tunic. Then, suddenly, Carrick saw what Doctor Hodson had meant by the 'magic wand routine'. Colour began returning to Page's face. His breathing steadied and strengthened, an arm stirred, an eyelid fluttered.

'Morphine derivative.' Hodson gave a satisfied grunt. 'Stay with him, Chief Officer. I'll try the girl now.'

He moved away, leaving Carrick to watch the tide of consciousness flow back. At last there was a groan, the fair-haired head twitched on the hospital pillow, and Page's eyes blinked open.

'Take it easy, John.' Carrick gave him a reassuring grin. 'You're in hospital.'

The words appeared to take time to percolate through. Then the young vet's mouth struggled to form a question.

'Aline's here,' confirmed Carrick. 'And –' he glanced across to the other bed and caught the doctor's nod of agreement – 'and she's all right.'

Page took a deep, sighing breath and lay still, only his eyes moving as he tried to take in his surroundings.

'Doctor?' Carrick waited for guidance.

Hodson crossed to the bedside. 'The girl's reacting, but she's taking longer, Chief Officer.' He scowled. 'I'd guess somebody with a fairly elementary knowledge shot the same dosage into each of them – non-fatal, but he forgot that her body-weight was a lot less which meant there'd be a greater effect.' He felt Page's pulse again, saw the young vet watching him, and nodded. 'Feel fit enough to talk now?'

'I – I'll manage,' said Page in a low, forced whisper.

'What did they use on you? The pure stuff?'

Page shook his head. 'Diambutene – quarter grain each. I – I gave him a supply of it a while back.'

'Veterinary drug,' growled Doctor Hodson for Carrick's benefit. 'A synthetic and a damned sight stronger than anything we use – animals have a high tolerance. You could shove eight times as much morphine as would kill a man into most dogs and they'd simply wag their tails at you. Still, the antidote's the same.' He winked at Page. 'You'll do. I'll get back to that good-looking young woman of yours'.

'Carrick . . .' Page swallowed, craning his head to watch as the doctor went back to the other bed. 'He's – he's sure about Aline?'

'She's taking longer, that's all,' soothed Carrick. 'You're in Mallaig. We found you after you'd been trans-shipped from Tenford's drifter.'

151

'Tenford!' Page jerked at the sound of the name. 'You've got him too?'

'Not yet, but we will.' Carrick watched him carefully. 'Tell me what happened, John.'

'Right.' Page forced a weak smile, the best indication of his gathering strength. 'A while back I – I wondered if I'd get the chance to tell anyone.' A thought struck him. 'What time is it?'

'About one-thirty, Friday afternoon.'

'Twelve hours –' Page winced. 'I remember coming round for a spell and knowing we were moving. They must have given us a second shot somewhere along the way.' He sighed. 'Well, where do I start?'

'At the cottage,' prompted Carrick. 'Why you weren't there when Arran got back. Tenford came visiting, didn't he?'

'Came and . . . and said he'd come to warn us about you asking questions, that you knew the cat had been out when the *Thrift* was raided.' Page started to struggle up on his elbows. 'Carrick, the reason –'

He eased him back on the pillow. 'We know about the liquor. Forget it. Did you tell Tenford about the bank daybooks?'

Page nodded. 'Aline showed them to him. He said they'd help clear us, that he was . . . was glad as a friend.' The word came bitterly. 'He went away, but he must have had some men over with him. They . . . two of them arrived minutes later, stuck a gun in Aline's back, and made us walk to the north shore, beyond the harbour bay. They had a boat there.'

'And on Buidhe? Where did they keep you?'

'In a cellar . . . at the house.' Page clenched his fists against the white bedsheets. 'Tenford came down and said he had to keep us out of circulation. We were carrying the can for the *Thrift* – and that was how he wanted it.'

'Did he say why?'

152

'No.' Page shook his head. 'Just that he was sorry but he needed time and we ... we could make it for him. Everything would have been fine if the *Thrift* hadn't been found, but they'd fouled up the job – that the way things were going it looked as if all he could do was play for time. I asked him about the *Thrift*'s crew, but he wouldn't answer. The next thing –' he frowned, tiring a little – 'something happened on Buidhe last night, some kind of trouble.'

'A couple of us paid a visit,' chuckled Carrick. 'Arran got us out of a messy situation.'

'Arran –' Page forced a smile. 'Aline wondered. Anyway, Tenford came down afterwards, in a rage. According to him, he'd got to get rid of us – and some of his pals thought it should be permanent.' The smile faded at the memory. 'We were going to be moved on the drifter, because nobody would look for us when it was doing a job for the Fishery Protection people. After that – he said he still didn't want to kill us, but it would depend on what happened. Then he brought out the diambutene, some I gave him a while back for a sick dog. He injected me first and –' he shrugged – 'that's all.'

Carrick bent closer. 'John, have you any idea what's going on out there?' As Page shook his head, he tried another tack. 'What about Tenford – what's his background?'

'Ordinary.' Page was openly weary. 'He joined his uncle's firm and worked with them until the old fellow died. I met him ... oh, years back. We kept in touch – that's how I met Aline, one time when I came over to visit him on Buidhe.'

A heavy hand pressed on Carrick's shoulder. He looked up, and Doctor Hodson shook his head then thumbed towards the door. Carrick followed him from the sideroom out into the corridor.

'He's done enough talking for now,' said Hodson briefly.

'Anyway, Inspector Muir's waiting in my office – down there, on the right.'

'How's the girl?' demanded Carrick.

'She'll do. I've got her on a second stage treatment, to perk up her breathing. They'll need a backing of antibiotic, but we can move them into the wards any time now. After that, all they'll need is rest, warmth and quiet.' He showed a slight impatience. 'Anything else?'

'One thing,' said Carrick slowly. 'Suppose somebody was given a smaller dose of this diambutene how would it affect him?'

'Depends on the dose. He could be happy, sleepy, semi-conscious – it's impossible to say.'

'Would it show in a post-mortem? If a man was found drowned, for instance?'

'That depends again – on who did the PM' Doctor Hodson nodded a curt farewell and disappeared back into the sideroom.

Inspector Muir was eager and willing to talk. He wheeled round from the window as Carrick entered the little office, the expression on his face strangely reminiscent of an excited, over-grown schoolboy.

'They're doing fine,' said Carrick. 'Page is conscious.'

'I know – Hodson told me.' Muir rubbed his hands together. 'Well, laddie, your drifter's sailed for Kenbeg and so far our two thugs from the launch are being stubborn. But I've got news for you, real news. Remember that leaf you brought over, the one from the greenhouse?'

'What about it?'

'We know Tenford's game, that's what – and it's a beauty! The Scientific team identified that leaf as *Cannabis indica* – marijuana! From the leaf size, they say it probably came from a young seedling. Webb, he must be growing the stuff wholesale!'

Marijuana – Carrick needed time to let it sink home. Hashish or bhang, dream weed, the drug had a dozen or more names. He'd seen it found when customs men raided a merchant ship in dock. He'd sniffed the sickly-sweet smoke it produced in a reefer cigarette, seen the way its users' sense of time and sound, reality and sanity, faded and died. That was when they'd boarded a cargo liner coming in from the Far East and had helped round up a trio of drug-crazed Indians who'd stabbed an officer then barricaded themselves in the fo'c'sle.

'According to the textbooks, all you do is grow the plant, dry it, then crush the lot down into powder,' said Muir excitedly. 'But you need the right climate – or Tenford's way. Got your motive now? Suppose Tenford was rendez-vousing with a ship, putting a cargo of marijuana aboard, and the *Thrift* wandered along and saw them – he'd panic. He'd know he couldn't let them get away and talk about it!'

He nodded, his mind grappling with possibilities. 'Maybe, Pete. Tenford was in his uncle's firm for years – they were in the patent medicine business, which means handling drugs.'

'So he'd know the ropes,' said Muir happily. 'Oh, and that other sample was pipe tobacco all right. But it doesn't matter much now, does it?'

'No.' Carrick automatically took out his cigarettes, lit one, and drew in the smoke. 'Pete, there's one thing wrong with that theory of yours. The drifter was in harbour the night the *Thrift* was raided.'

Muir shrugged. 'So they used another boat. I've some-thing else, not vital but it helps. The truck we found at Balbeg has been seen around the district before – we fol-lowed that up, and backtracked it to a holiday cottage on a side-road about five miles inland, near Loch Morar. There's a barn behind the cottage that's been used as a garage – and a two-way radio in the cottage itself.'

155

Carrick was barely listening. 'Did the drifter crew show any worry when I didn't turn up?'

Muir shook his head. 'They were told the story that you'd received fresh orders. They seemed happy enough as long as they got away – the sea's roughening up.'

'There's a gale forecast for tonight,' agreed Carrick absently. 'Pete, neither Page nor the girl will be fit to travel for a spell. But I've got to get back out there.'

'Eh? To Kenbeg, you mean?' Muir scratched his head. 'Well now, let's see –' He suddenly snapped his fingers. 'There's the *Lochcraig*, the Outer Isles mail steamer. She's due here from the south within the hour, and she sails about four. She's fast, and Kenbeg wouldn't be too far off her course.'

'Fix it any way you can,' Carrick told him. 'And while you're doing it, I'll get a signal through to *Marlin*. I want Captain Shannon to know the picture and be ready when the drifter arrives.'

No mailboat will lightly alter schedule – and the threatened gale was a factor no captain could afford to ignore. But whatever tactics Muir employed, whatever appeals he made, Carrick was aboard the *Lochcraig* when she sailed. Behind him lay a series of coded messages to and from *Marlin*, sent out on the Fishery Service reserve wave length, one far removed from the normal shipping band or the likelihood of being picked up by anyone who might read a significance into their length and number.

He travelled on the *Lochcraig's* bridge, in itself a jealously granted privilege. He shared a dram from the captain's bottle, heard the *Lochcraig's* tannoy system advise her passengers of a 'necessary additional call', then watched, an interested spectator, while the mailboat's powerful twin screw beat drove her hard and fast towards the west. The Inner Isles fell rapidly astern of her long

156

white wash while the gradually rising wind snatched and swept away the smoke from her distinctive twin funnels.

As dusk fell the sea's face showed an angry change. The long, deepening swell became more broken, white wave-crests clashing one against the other, the mailboat occasionally shuddering as her bow dipped in a trough and her stern rose high. Her engines crept back a few revolutions and the crew went round clamping down the last porthole deadlights, roping off exposed sections of companionway, double-checking the lashings on hatches and deck cargo.

By eight o'clock the *Lochcraig* was travelling through pitch-dark night with seas breaking high over her bow and a windblown mixture of sleet and rain battering her from above. But on the bridge all was calm – bad weather was routine on the mailboat run. And a little later, her captain handed Carrick his glasses and pointed ahead. A darker silhouette against the night, the Rathbeg Isles lay about a mile ahead.

A light began bobbing out towards them from the Kenbeg channel, a light which became a lobster boat, tossing in the waves, seeking round to the lee side as the mailboat gradually slowed to a crawl. The gap narrowed, the little boat bobbed alongside, and one of the three people aboard waved a greeting. Carrick said his goodbyes, scrambled down a rope ladder, then jumped. A strong arm caught him and dragged him aboard the tiny craft, her engine quickened, and she surged away from the towering steel of the *Lochcraig's* hull.

'Helluva night,' bellowed Clapper Bell, grinning from under the hood of his oilskins. 'Here, better put this on, sir.'

Carrick fumbled his way into the spare set of oilskins. The mailboat was already curving away from them, heading back on her scheduled route. Her passengers were going to curse the bad weather ahead of them – curse it and the unknown reason for their delay.

157

'What's been happening, Clapper?'

'Plenty,' shouted Bell above the noise of the wind. 'An' it's not finished. *Marlin's* out after the drifter, but the Old Man left me an' some o' the lads to help the cops raid Buidhe.' He beamed from ear to ear at the memory. 'Still, there's a couple o' folk who're more needin' to talk to you than I am.' He pointed towards the stern.

Carrick looked, recognized the two figures huddled in the scanty shelter of the low cockpit, and scrambled towards them. Arran MacKenna and her father were cold and damp, but they greeted him with a warmth and urgency.

'Aline and the lad – they're all right, like you told Shannon?' demanded MacKenna, gripping him tight by the hand.

'Doing fine,' confirmed Carrick, his voice loud as another wave broke against the bow, drenching them with spray. 'Rest is all they'll need.'

'Aye.' An expression of relief split the older man's face. He took one hand from the steering wheel and ran it happily through his white hair, pushing back the hood on his oilskins. 'Man, I'm not the praying kind, but I've said a few this day.'

'Webb –' Arran pressed close against him as the boat lurched. She didn't try to move back, she let her eyes say the rest.

He put an arm round her waist and if Sawny MacKenna noticed, the fisherman gave no sign. 'Clapper says they've raided Buidhe. Did they get Tenford?'

'No.' Her mouth tightened fractionally. 'Wait until we get in – it's a long story.'

Things were quieter once the lobster boat gained the shelter of the channel. She throbbed her way through to the harbour bay, they tied up alongside the pier, then wasted no time in clambering off. Rain-soaked but resolute, Chief Inspector Dawe's tall, thin figure greeted them as they stepped ashore.

'Let's get out of this,' he said quickly, huddling deep into his coat. 'Otherwise I'm going to die of pneumonia or worse.' Carrick needed no urging. Like the others, he hustled along the pier and through the village to MacKenna's cottage. Dawe was the last to enter. He slammed the door shut behind him, shook the rain from his hat-brim, then let his face shape into an unaccustomed friendliness. 'Glad you're back, Carrick. MacKenna's letting us use his place as an office – and that includes having a fire and a coffee pot.'

They hung coats and oilskins on the row of pegs in the hall and went into the front room. The transceiver set hummed gently in its corner, giving out an occasional crackle of static. Detective Sergeant Wylie moved his bulk from the warmth of the blazing fire in the hearth, nodded a greeting, and began pouring coffee from a heavy metal pot into an assortment of cups and mugs. Then, as they grouped around the fire, clothes gently steaming in the heat, he handed out the scalding hot liquid.

'Thanks.' Carrick sipped from his mug and glanced towards Dawe. 'Chief Inspector –'

'You want to know what's happened.' Dawe gave a small, not completely happy nod. 'Right. Shannon and I decided to let the drifter come in and get my extra men ashore before we did anything. While we were waiting, we turned MacKenna loose. We –' he kept a tight restraint on his choice of words – 'we told him a few things about himself in the process.'

'You certainly did, Chief Inspector.' Arran chuckled at the memory.

Dawe blushed a little, saw Sergeant Wylie grinning from near the window, and threw him a glare. 'Anyway, the drifter came in just before dusk. She landed my men, then moored as usual in the bay. We were ready to move in as soon as it was dark – but then that damned boat upset things by heading out to sea again!'

Carrick whistled and glanced sideways at Clapper Bell.

159

'She was in for less than half an hour, sir,' agreed the bo'sun. 'I kept the glasses on her. One man took a dinghy over to Buidhe, an' two rowed back to her after a spell.'

'Even if Tenford wasn't personally making a bolt for it we thought there must be some pretty urgent reason for her going out,' said Dawe unhappily. 'Shannon left me any men he could spare and followed. He's shadowing on radar, and so far they're heading north.'

'But now you don't think Tenford's aboard,' said Carrick bluntly.

It brought a sardonic grunt from Sawny MacKenna and a wince from the policeman. 'It looks that way,' admitted Dawe. 'Once *Marlin* had sailed we raided Buidhe and rounded up every man we could find. Tenford and three of his men are still missing, yet I'll guarantee they're not on that island.'

'And the ones you've got?'

'Ach, some are just plain, honest gardeners,' explained Clapper Bell, crossing to the table and helping himself to another mug of coffee. 'The others – well, there was a wee scuffle or two but nothin' to get excited about.'

The Chief Inspector stared mournfully at the cup in his hand. 'That's how it is. There was a legitimate business operation going on side-by-side with the marijuana project. But this is what matters, Carrick. As far as I can make out Tenford didn't sail on that drifter – he disappeared after it had gone.'

'After he'd sent it out as a decoy – and I can guess the reason.' Carrick inwardly cursed for not having thought of it earlier. 'Tenford would be expecting a radio call from the mainland to report Aline and Page had been delivered without trouble. But we picked up the men who'd have to send that signal – he'd know something had gone wrong.' But there was still a gap, a gap which only one long-shot possibility could fill. 'Arran, what other boats were on Buidhe?'

160

'Only small stuff,' she said without hesitation. 'Nothing much bigger than a rowing boat.'

'Nothing he could risk in open water on a night like this,' rumbled her father.

'Yet this happened before,' said Carrick savagely. 'The drifter didn't leave Kenbeg on the night the *Thrift* was attacked. What about it, Dawe? Did you find anything on Buidhe that might hold an answer?'

'Sergeant . . .' Dawe beckoned, and Wylie ambled over with a brown paper package in one hand. 'This is all so far – the banking daybooks from the *Thrift* with MacKenna's withdrawal noted.' He sighed. 'We checked that greenhouse, of course – and it's stacked full of marijuana seedlings though nobody admits knowing a damned thing about them. And, if you're interested, Wylie located a storeman who issued a couple of tins of rat poison to Drammy MacPherson – on Tenford's instructions.'

Wylie grunted and broke his silence. 'That's what killed your oysters, MacKenna. Could be that Tenford liked stirring up trouble so that no-one had time to bother about what he was doing.'

Sawny MacKenna shook his head in a sad bewilderment.

'MacPherson still matters.' Carrick lapsed into silence for a moment. 'He could be part of the reason why the *Thrift* was attacked.'

'Eh?' Dawe raised an incredulous eyebrow. 'MacPherson was dead by then!'

'Perris only said it looked that way,' countered Carrick. 'He was careful enough not to tie himself down to any exact time. Tenford used a heavy dose of diambutene on Aline and Page. But a smaller amount would leave a man groggy, probably too groggy to struggle if he was dumped into the sea.'

'A drug would have shown in the PM –'

'You'd have a body with all the expected signs of accidental drowning.' Carrick spoke slowly and deliberately. 'A second examination would be unlikely – and even if there was, our Doctor Perris could wriggle out by saying he'd made all the tests that seemed necessary to back his findings.'

'But you're not so sure it would be a mistake, is that it?' Sawny MacKenna frowned uneasily. 'Doctor Perris has done a lot of good work around these islands.'

'Think for a moment,' urged Carrick. 'He has the *Emma-Dee*, a boat that can face most weather. He turns up at Kenbeg on the same morning your girls go lobster-fishing – turns up unexpectedly as far as anyone but Tenford is concerned. Tenford knew the girls were going out – and if he knew they'd find MacPherson's body what could be handier than having Perris on the spot to take care of the post-mortem?' He saw the protest forming on Dawe's lips. 'Sorry, Chief Inspector, but I'm betting that's the reason Perris paid us a visit – just as I'm betting that Tenford wanted MacPherson found near Kenbeg for reasons of his own.' He swung round on Clapper Bell. 'When did Perris sail from here?'

'This mornin', early on. He said he was goin' north, to some fishing village.'

'Ardallan on Uist,' snapped Dawe. 'He told me yesterday.'

'Maybe Perris came back,' said Carrick softly. 'Tenford could have radioed him and arranged a rendezvous on the far side of Buidhe –'

'Then sent out the drifter as a decoy.' Dawe groaned aloud and for a moment looked almost ill. 'It's – no, I'm with you for once. It could make sense. We'll have to warn Shannon.'

Carrick nodded. 'Clapper, that's your job. First call is to *Marlin*. Tell the Old Man to –' he corrected himself with a flicker of a grin – 'submit to him that he arrests the drifter right away. After that, get a message through to Mallaig police. That bank investigator Campbell said he was an old pal of Wilson, the *Thrift's* manager. I want to know if

Wilson had any hobby interest in botany – there were a couple of books on it in his cabin.'

'Right, sir.' The Petty Officer started to cross to the radio then hesitated. 'What about Perris?'

'That's the third job. Try to check whether he reached Ardallan, and if he did, where he went from there.'

'We've wasted more than two hours, two hours with *Marlin* shadowing that damned boat,' said Dawe bitterly. 'Now what?'

'Let's wait for some answers.' Carrick gave a bleak grimace. 'I'm going to see MacPherson's mother. I know – she's unreliable. But right now she's all we've got.'

'I'd like to come with you,' said MacKenna almost apologetically. 'There was a time when she counted me a friend. Now – well, she tells the truth as she believes it. There's a black debt between us, Carrick, one I've got to pay any way I can.'

Carrick shook his head. 'You stay, Sawny. What you do later is your own affair, but not now.'

Chapter Eight

The night was a black howl of battering wind and drenching rain. Outside the cottage, Webb Carrick hesitated a moment while his eyes became accustomed to the darkness, then fought a stumbling path down towards the beach. From there, he followed its edge towards the old hulk of the *Silver Queen*.

As he plodded on, the rain pattering hard and fast against his oilskins, the crash of waves against the shore held a new, menacing undertone – a rattling growl as the sea sucked against the shingle, pulling it down with one retreating breaker, throwing it back again with the next. But when he reached the old fishing boat a faint light glowed behind its portholes and Jean MacPherson soon opened the makeshift door in response to his knocking.

He went in, and she quickly shut and barred the door. The dull light came from two smoking kerosene lamps – and he saw she was dressed in mourning black, old-fashioned, smelling of mothballs, still showing the crumpled creasing of years of storage.

'A wild night, Mr Carrick,' she said wearily. 'No night to be out.'

Carrick nodded, loosening the oilskins but getting no invitation to remove them. He noticed other changes in the woman – and her surroundings. The grey hair was neatly combed, the lace-edged, yellowed handkerchief tucked into one sleeve of her dress was clean and carefully folded, and there was a strange, almost hypnotic dignity about her bearing. A pathetic attempt had been made to tidy the ramshackle cabin and the silver-framed photograph stood proud in the centre of the table, a small posy of wild flowers resting beside it in a water-filled cup. Mourning had its own ritual in the islands, a ritual and a discipline bred into its people, sustaining in its depth – whatever might come later.

'You'll be here about my boy?'

'Just one or two more questions, Mrs MacPherson,' he told her.

She met his gaze with dull eyes which didn't blink. 'His body should be here, Mr Carrick. As his mother, I have my duty.'

'I know.' He shifted his feet awkwardly. 'But the police would explain their reasons –'

She nodded, but said nothing.

'It's about the night he took the *Mora* –'

'When folk say he went stealing from the MacKenna girls' creels.' Suddenly her eyes came angrily to life. 'Not my Archie! All the rest of the things they say he did to their father – I knew about them. But not to the girls. They did us no harm, not them and not their mother.'

'That's why I've come,' said Carrick, his voice gentle. 'I need help, Mrs MacPherson, help in trying to understand why your son died. We're just beginning to find out other things, things which alter the situation.'

'Like what happened to the girl Aline – I heard from the village.' She turned towards the stove, her lips tight. The stove burned a fierce red behind its metal bars, but even so the draughts whistling through the boat's broken, neglected hull left the air bitterly cold.

'Your son had been drinking,' reminded Carrick in the same quiet, steady fashion. 'Supposing the result was he wanted to get away for a spell, wanted to be by himself –'

'That happened sometimes.' The woman seemed barely conscious of his presence. 'He'd stand where you are, the whisky in his mind but a misery in his heart, and then he'd go off.'

'Go where?'

She looked at him tiredly. 'Go to try to be like his father, to try the great lines.'

'By himself?' Carrick stared at her incredulously. For one man, even an expert, to go great-line fishing was a bold venture. For that man to be a stumbling drunk came close to attempted suicide.

She nodded. 'Just himself with some old bits of line and rusted hooks – like a child, a child trying to find something he needed.'

'Like happiness?'

Her lips stayed together but her mouth twitched.

'Where would he go, Mrs MacPherson?'

'The first place the Kenbeg boats looked – the same place his father often went.' Her eyes were moist now, and she tried to hide the fact.

'The Abbey Isles, Mrs MacPherson?'

'Yes.' She took a deep breath. 'There was always good fishing there, for those like his father who knew the marks.'

'Did Dra— Did your son know the marks?'

She shook her head. 'No, but he went – he always hoped, Mr Carrick.'

'Thank you.' He began refastening the oilskins and moved towards the door. Suddenly, he felt her hand on his arm.

'That girl, Mr Carrick – her and the lad she's to marry. How are they?'

'Still in hospital, but doing well.'

For a moment a struggle seemed to go on within her. Then she nodded. 'I'm glad. Will you take a message to her father?'

'I'm going back to meet him.'

'Then tell him –' she hesitated – 'tell him I am glad she will be well.'

166

'Anything else?'

She unbolted the door. 'Should there be, Mr Carrick?'

He shook his head and went out into the night. Jean MacPherson was a lonely woman, a lost woman. For her there would never be a fairy-tale ending, whatever other people hoped.

Sawny MacKenna's cottage was strangely empty when he got back. Only MacKenna and Chief Inspector Dawe were in the front room, but he sensed an air of taut excitement shared between them – sensed it and saw confirmation in the hard, purposeful gleam in Dawe's eyes.

'*Marlin's* got the drifter,' said the policeman without any preliminaries. 'Captain Shannon called us back a matter of minutes ago – they closed and boarded. Tenford wasn't on her, but the four men aboard are under arrest and a prize crew is taking over. He's turning round and making all speed back here.'

Carrick grinned. When Shannon said 'all speed' it meant that everything including the safety valves would be tied down to pull extra power from the fishery cruiser. 'Fine.' He glanced around. 'Where's everybody gone?'

'Sergeant Wylie is away to see how things are on Buidhe,' volunteered MacKenna. He gave a loose grin. 'Your bo'sun went off to give Arran a help with a wee job.'

'Oh?' Carrick raised an eyebrow, but there was no explanation forthcoming. 'Any word from Mallaig?'

'From Mallaig and from Ardallan,' growled Dawe. 'Campbell confirms the *Thrift's* manager was an amateur botanist – meaning, I suppose, he could have identified marijuana if he saw it. The word back from Ardallan is that Perris arrived there, saw a few patients, then left in a hurry early this afternoon saying he'd received an emergency call. He headed the *Emma-Dee* south.'

'In this direction,' murmured MacKenna. 'I did a wee bit asking around the village, Carrick. One of the lobster

167

boats spotted the *Emma-Dee* about five o'clock this evening. She was about ten miles out, travelling fast, still heading for here.'

Dawe prowled the room in restless fashion, stopped beside the transceiver, and tapped his fingers on the metal top. 'But it's not enough. We've got to come up with some kind of a lead for Shannon. He can't start combing the entire Hebridean chain on the chance he'll spot her.'

'There's a hell of a lot of water out there,' agreed Carrick amiably. 'But my money's on the Abbey Isles. Mrs MacPherson says that's where Drammy probably took the *Mora*.'

Dawe gave a wry, unhappy grimace. 'All right, I'll listen.'

Carrick settled himself in one of the big chairs by the fireside, his legs stretched out to the heat. 'We know the *Thrift* was somewhere near the Abbey Isles the night after Drammy took the *Mora*. One way and another we've got up to three other boats reported around there that night. One was Page's catamaran with you aboard, MacKenna. Let's say another was your Irish smuggling pal, but that he decided it was too busy a patch of ocean and went home again. The third boat –'

'The *Emma-Dee*, waiting to contact another kind of smuggler,' said Dawe viciously. 'A barrel or two of liquor's one thing, but drugs –' He gave a throaty growl of contempt.

'I wasn't thinking of a contact,' said Carrick almost reproachfully. 'There was a heavy sea running, almost as bad as tonight's. Suppose the *Thrift* tucked into shelter at the Isles, suppose there was a reason why Wilson her manager went ashore, a reason like Drammy MacPherson –'

A sudden light dawned on MacKenna's face. 'Man, that could be it – if he'd been wrecked and got ashore the previous night!'

Dawe watched them with a wary, sceptical silence.

168

'Wilson might have been interested in what he found,' mused Carrick. 'Particularly if he stumbled across a crop of marijuana.'

'Eh?' Both men stared at him incredulously.

He nodded with a quiet, rock-hard conviction. Almost all the facts had been in their grasp, waiting. But knowing them separately and seeing them suddenly mesh together were very different propositions. 'Dawe, you say all the marijuana plants on Buidhe are seedlings. That has to mean the adult plants are grown somewhere else, somewhere warm enough and yet completely safe. The Abbey Isles are like plenty of other spots around here, slap in the middle of the Gulf Stream – and the Gulf Stream means warmth.' He leaned forward in the chair. 'Look, I hardly know one plant from another. But I've seen places on this coast where roses bloom at Christmas even though there's ice and snow lying thick a mile away. I've seen palm trees and tropical gardens, things that sound impossible but exist.'

Dawe swallowed hard. One of the biggest tourist attractions in his own county area was one of those tropical gardens, run by the National Trust at Inverewe. 'So they take a group of empty, uninhabited islands and –' He winced. 'Hell, this could have been going on for years!'

'Tenford and Perris aren't fools.' Carrick's thoughts were far ahead now. 'But between making sure MacPherson's body was found near here, taking the *Thrift* well out to sea before they tried to scuttle her and now this game with the drifter, they probably feel the Abbey Isles are relatively safe – safe enough to head there and collect any marijuana they've got in store.'

'A few sacks of the stuff and they can buy a one-way ticket anywhere they want.' Dawe pursed his lips. 'The quicker we contact *Marlin* the better.'

Sawny MacKenna scratched his head. 'Aye, but it'll be another couple of hours and more before she can be down at the Abbeys. Perris' boat would have a rough time in this

169

weather, but even so she'll be there by now – and maybe gone by the time *Marlin* arrives.' He eyed them hopefully. 'Now, we're a lot nearer, if you take my meaning. Not much more than twenty miles away – we could be there in an hour or so.'

'Using what?' asked Carrick bluntly.

'Well, the lobster boats are too slow,' admitted the old fisherman. 'But there's one boat left in Kenbeg that's fast enough – John Page's catamaran. She'd have the wind behind her almost all the way.'

'The *Gooshgash*?' Carrick hesitated. The cat had the speed, could cope with the weather better than most – but there was still a problem. 'Who'd handle her sails? I'm no yachtsman.'

'Arran,' said MacKenna, a sudden sureness and authority in his voice. 'Those girls of mine have crewed that boat with Page in plenty of races. There are few better, Carrick – and Arran is down at the pier right now with that bo'sun of yours, making sure everything's ready. We had a feeling the *Gooshgash* might be needed for something like this.'

'But –'

'She knows the boat,' emphasized MacKenna. 'I'll be aboard too – but I'll do what she tells me.'

There was no alternative. 'All right,' said Carrick reluctantly. 'Add Clapper Bell and myself and that's four.'

'Five,' said Dawe briefly. 'I'm coming.'

Carrick looked at him for a moment then shook his head. 'No, not you, Chief Inspector. Once we stick our noses outside this bay we hit the real storm – and the way it's building up any passengers would be a liability.'

'Hell, I could always make the ruddy tea,' declared Dawe stubbornly.

'Somebody's got to run things here,' Carrick told him. 'You've got your job, we've got ours.'

Dawe glared, then gave a long sigh. 'I'd probably have been as sick as a dog,' he confessed. 'But –'

'But now we're wasting time,' said MacKenna quickly. 'Webb, if you use that wee radio of mine to tell *Marlin* what we're doing that should make us just about ready.' He cocked his head towards Dawe. 'Chief Inspector, if there was a man you knew who had a rifle he'd forgotten to licence would it worry you?'

'It would.' Dawe grunted. 'I'd be worried in case he'd forgotten where he'd hidden the ammunition.'

Snug in the quilted waterproof of her dark blue sailing jacket, the draw-strings of the hood pulled tight so that it formed a warm oval framing her face, Arran MacKenna took the helm as the *Gooshgash* headed down-channel from the bay towards the open sea. She used the cat's outboard engine for convenience until they were in mid-channel, then, her eyes watchful in the glow of the tiny lamp on the compass binnacle, lost no time in changing to the sail-power from which the boat would draw her greatest pace.

Mainsail and jib, the vast crimson balloon spinnaker and a smaller spinnaker staysail – Carrick and Bell worked side by side with Sawny MacKenna, guided through the complexity of stays and halliards by Arran's crisp, shouted instructions. Above their heads, the big nylon sails billowed and rippled as the gusting wind-currents seized them, then filled taut and hard as the last sheets were secured.

The job was completed just before they reached the mouth of the channel, and the three men clambered back into the cockpit moments before the first of the heavy seas beyond lashed hungrily against the *Gooshgash*, smashing in a fury against her portside hull. Coolly, a faint almost welcoming smile on her lips, Arran eased the helm round until sea and wind were almost dead astern. The sails crackled briefly, the wind met their obstruction with a furious force which sent a brief vibration running down the length of the long tubular mainmast – and the cat was running free, halliards creaking, her twin bows almost planing through the turbulent water.

Carrick gripped the cockpit rail as a fresh curtain of fine spray drenched aboard, watching the girl sway with the boat's lurch, all the assurance of a ballet dancer in her fine sense of balance, her attention constantly switching between sails and compass.

'MacKenna –' He had to shout a second time, almost in the fisherman's ear, to get his attention. 'That's one devil of a lot of sail we're carrying.'

'She knows what she's doing,' declared MacKenna bluntly. 'Leave her be, man.'

She heard them and glanced around. 'The *Gooshgash* can take it, Webb, better than most. John says he once got twenty knots out of her – we'll see if he's right.'

He winced as another great sea reared astern of them, lifted the cat almost bodily, then slammed hard directly beneath them as it was trapped between the twin hulls.

Still she was unperturbed. 'We can hold it for now. If we have to, we'll reef in the mainsail and use a storm jib – but not yet.'

The next hour was a test of endurance, despite the cat's twin-hulled stability in conditions which would have made most vessels twice her size heave to and attempt to ride out the weather.

Twice they had to struggle to slacken the spinnaker when a rising fury of wind threatened to bury her bows, a fury which, unchecked, would have heaved the *Gooshgash* stern over bow and left them struggling for life in a wilderness of angry water. Once, disaster threatened in a different way – as a freak, twisting squall struck them on the port side and the cat lurched over on her lee hull until its twin was almost clear of the water. Then, suddenly, she levelled out – and as water swirled and gurgled from the self-draining cockpit Carrick saw Arran's hands were gripping the helm knuckle-white.

172

But they were travelling – the log indicator showed nineteen knots most of the way and clicked busily to twenty-two for one brief spell. And the lashing rain from above had stopped, the clouds became more ragged, and there was even an occasional glimpse of moonlight.

Sawny MacKenna strained his eyes ahead, peering through the drenching flurries of driving spindrift, silent, gnawing his lip. But at last he grinned and slapped one hand on the cockpit rail.

'On ahead – see it?'

A minute later they did – a small white light which blinked and vanished, blinked again.

'The Abbot's Light, girl,' he told his daughter exultantly. 'The automatic beacon at the north end of the Isles.'

Carrick watched the light flash again then peered at the luminous dial of his watch. Less than an hour had passed since they'd cleared Kenbeg.

'On time and course – nice goin'!' Clapper Bell grinned. 'What now, eh?'

Carrick crowded closer to the binnacle light and squinted down at the folded chart he'd found among the selection in Page's locker. He guessed the beacon to be about a mile ahead, and he'd already worked out their next move.

Scattered on the chart in a rough, haphazard curve, the Abbey Isles were eight in number. High-cliffed relics of some volcanic incident of prehistory, only two had ever been inhabited – the others were mere monoliths of black basalt rock, scanty in soil and vegetation. The two that mattered were near the middle of the group. The smaller of these, Abbot's Isle, still possessed a few fragmentary ruins of the early Christian abbey which had given the group its name and the chart showed an anchorage with deep water. But Nettri, next in the curve, larger, once supporting a village of some twenty families until the mainland's pull had left a handful of pensioners to die out

173

long years past, was low-lying and had a vestige of an old stone jetty.

'We come in like this –' His thumbnail traced over the paper, keeping the beacon light to port and skirting in to the west of Abbot's Isle. 'As long as we don't go in close and the cloud keeps that moonlight blanked we'll be all right. If we see anything, Clapper and I go in with the dinghy.'

'Eh?' MacKenna's mouth gaped. 'Hell, man, it's no' much more than an eggbox. You wouldn't last a minute.'

'We'll have the island between us and the worst of the gale.' Even so, he knew it wouldn't be easy. But Clapper Bell's confident nod showed that he, at any rate, felt it was a gamble worth backing.

'Why risk it?' objected Arran, her voice sharp and troubled, yet almost lost against the wind. 'We could take the *Gooshgash* right in.'

'And chance that we all run smack into trouble?' Carrick shook his head. 'This way makes more sense.'

She still didn't like it. But gradually, gauging her action by the feel of the wind in her face, she eased the helm round and kept the cat eating away to leeward until they were running with the beacon light to port.

Five minutes later, navigation lights blacked out, her sail reduced to a small storm jib and a close-reefed mainsail, the *Gooshgash* tacked into the sheltered lee of Abbot's Isle. Lying about half a mile out, the cat heaved in the heavy, rolling swell while Carrick trained the cockpit glasses on the shore.

The moonlight broke through briefly. He swept the length of the pebbled beach, caught a glimpse of the broken ruin of the old abbey, but could see no sign of life.

They steered on for Nettri. Above them, another vast bank of cloud swarmed across the sky and, as they cleared the shelter of Abbot's Isle, an angry squall of wind and sea raged around them, lashing the water into a wild, silver-flecked cauldron. Spray drenched over the cockpit combing, rigging groaned and creaked with the strain – then once again they were in calmer water and Carrick scanned the shore.

'Well?' demanded MacKenna.

Carrick kept his eyes against the glasses for almost another minute. But when he turned he gave a tight, thin-lipped grin of triumph. 'They're there – I can't pick out the *Emma-Dee*, but there are lights moving near the old quay.'

Reluctantly MacKenna moved forward and began loosening the dinghy's lashings while Carrick and Clapper Bell stripped off their oilskins and removed their heavy seaboots. If the dinghy went over, swimming would be a tough enough business without that kind of extra weight.

'For any sake's be careful,' urged MacKenna. 'We'll be watching, but even so –' He shook his head uneasily.

They lowered the little dinghy into the water, then, as it heaved alongside, Clapper Bell scrambled aboard. Carrick hesitated for a moment as Arran left the cockpit. Her lips moved, but the words were lost in the wind. He squeezed her gently by the arm, nodded to MacKenna, slid down into the dinghy, and shoved it clear. Clapper Bell already had the oars unshipped and began pulling.

If there had been worrying moments aboard the *Gooshgash* in the open water, the dinghy's behaviour in comparative shelter was still wild enough. Several times only the sheer brute muscle-power exerted by the burly giant at her oars swung the boat round fast enough to prevent some white-trimmed broken-angled wave from broaching their gunwale and throwing them over.

The shore loomed ahead as they rose on the crest of one massive breaker – then, suddenly, they were riding in on the next, trapped in its grip. It smashed down, and they were thrown out in a mad tumble, clawing for a grip on the rocks, fighting off the fierce under-tow, being pushed shoreward again by another breaker.

175

Battered, bruised, soaked to the skin, they at last picked themselves up. The dinghy had likewise been thrown ashore, upturned, but intact, one oar lying beside it, the other jammed in a crevice of rock a little way distant. They righted the boat, dragged it clear and, once the oars had been collected, stood shivering while they found their bearings. They'd come ashore about five hundred yards to the west of Nettri village.

'There's what we want,' hissed Clapper Bell, pointing. The black silhouette of the *Emma-Dee* was now clearly visible, moored snug against the tiny quay. 'If I got a couple o' minutes to mysel' over there, I could fix things good an' proper as far as her ever leaving is concerned.'

Carrick held him back. 'They'll have left a guard aboard. But the lights came from somewhere in the village. We'll try there first.'

Clothes clinging to their bodies like a chill second skin, they found it a relief to start moving. Once they'd reached the outskirts of the cluster of abandoned cottages they travelled more cautiously, keeping to the deepest shadow.

'Hold it –' Carrick breathed a warning as he saw a faint glow of yellowed light coming through the cracks of a shuttered window on ahead. Next moment, the door of the cottage swung open, light cut across the pebbled pathway, and a man came out, carrying a bulky sack over one shoulder. As the door slammed shut behind him he bent his head against the storm and began to trudge towards the quay.

They stole forward. The window shutter, warped and loose, creaked and groaned with the wind as Carrick peered through a crack.

Inside, a battery lamp lit a small room. Another lamp shone beyond, through an opened inner door. The small room was empty, apart from a bundle of folded sacks lying on its stone flagged floor. As he watched, a man emerged from the inner room, carrying the second lamp in one hand and dragging a filled sack with the other. He put

176

down the lamp, shouldered the sack, and, guessing what was coming, the two watchers slipped farther back into the shadows. The cottage door opened, the man came out, looked casually around, then, closing the door, headed off with his burden in the same direction as his predecessor.

'Want him?' queried Clapper Bell hoarsely.

'No. Play sentry for me.'

The cottage door squeaked open at Carrick's touch and he went in, picked up one of the lamps, and headed for the inner room. A soft whistle escaped through his teeth – the room was filled with layer upon layer of dry, coarse, yellow-brown stalks of marijuana leaf. This was Tenford's storeroom and, wherever else the drying plant might be located, Carrick gauged there must be half a ton of the drug's raw material lying around. One corner had been almost cleared, a powdered remnant of twigs and fragments trampled underfoot.

A quick, warning tap on the outside door stopped him searching further. He put the lamp back where he'd found it, carefully closed the cottage door as he left, and Clapper Bell quickly hauled him back round the angle of the building.

'There's a light comin' this way,' growled Bell.

The light came nearer, two men behind it. As the cottage door was shoved open, the leading figure was plainly visible – Doctor Perris, a scowl on his face, a trenchcoat tightly belted round his ample middle. The other – as the door slammed shut, Carrick had a vague memory of the man from his first visit to Buidhe.

'Leave them,' he murmured. 'Let's have a look at what's going on down by the quay.'

They edged past the cottage and were about two hundred yards beyond it on the way to the shore when a voice bellowed behind them. A second shout was followed by the lancing beam of one of the battery lamps. It found them, steadied, and a shot rang out, the bullet whining off the pathway near their feet. Carrick cursed. The water still dripping from his clothes, falling on that dry stone floor – he'd been a fool, and now it looked as if they'd pay the penalty.

'Start running – head for the dinghy!' He urged his companion on, then followed. Two more shots blasted out in quick succession and whined overhead as they rounded a broken wall and the light lost them.

'Watch it –' Clapper Bell's warning came just as he saw the figure of a man standing in a half-crouch only yards ahead. Orange flame flared and the bo'sun staggered as the shot rang out. But the big Petty Officer kept going – and the second shot went skywards as he bore the gunman down. Carrick saw the gun swinging round again as the two men rolled – but a dull glint of steel flashed in Bell's hand and the man beneath him kicked once and went limp. Clapper Bell rolled clear, the blade of his diving knife stained dark along its length as he shoved it back in his waist-sheath.

'Him or me.' Bell winced as Carrick dragged him to his feet. 'Easy – it's my leg he got.'

They heard shouts behind them. Quickly, half-supporting Clapper Bell, Carrick hustled him into the maze of cottages. They saw lights shining behind them – but for the moment they'd lost their pursuers.

Clapper Bell was staggering blindly by the time they reached the dinghy. Carrick helped him aboard, shoved the boat down to the water's edge, chose his time, then, as one combing breaker smashed ashore, shoved the boat off into its back-lash. The dinghy was sucked out – and in seconds he was aboard, rowing with a straining, desperate urgency as the next wave attempted to hustle them back in.

Somehow, he got clear. Fingers digging into the wood of the oars, he began fighting the dinghy out from the shore, conscious of the torches moving along the beach. One swept out, caught the dinghy in its glare, and held it. A single shot rang out, but no more – the wildly bobbing boat made an impossible target.

Carrick kept rowing, putting distance between boat and shore, ears straining for the inevitable.

It came soon, the growl of the motor-boat's engines starting up. A harsh white finger of light stabbed out as the *Emma-Dee's* wheelhouse spotlight was switched on, and the engine note rose as she headed out from the quay. Sweat beading on his forehead yet his hands so cold they'd lost almost all feeling, Carrick pulled on at the same gruelling mechanical rhythm. The spotlight swung, passed them, but came back again, pinning the dinghy in its powerful glare. He saw Clapper Bell's face twisted in pain, his eyes fixed on Carrick, one hand pressed hard against his left thigh. The motor-boat's bow turned, and began lurching through the swell towards them.

He gasped for breath – then in amazed delight as a new, far brighter light burst in the sky directly over the other boat. The flare burned its blinding, incandescent fury for long seconds – and before it sputtered out the motor-boat was swinging away, its spotlight suddenly extinguished.

'Where is she?' demanded Clapper Bell hoarsely, hauling himself up. 'How the hell did the Old Man manage –' He stopped, his mouth hanging open, as the throb of another, lighter engine reached their ears. It was no fishery cruiser that was approaching.

The dark-hulled catamaran clawed down towards them, her mainsail tumbled as she swung round to bring the dinghy under her lee – and then they had bumped alongside, and Carrick found himself helping MacKenna to drag Clapper Bell aboard, then scrambling up after him, leaving the dinghy to float away.

At the helm, Arran was already gunning the engine and steering the cat round to gain the wind once more. MacKenna pointed urgently to the flapping sails.

179

'Give me a hand,' he barked. 'That outboard couldn't pull the skin off a rice pudding – quick, man, if you want to get out of this.'

Carrick sprang to join him. Overhead, the cloud was breaking again and in a few moments there would be moonlight. First the mainsail rose and filled, then the running jib bellied out. As the wind bit greedily, Arran killed the engine and held the helm hard down. Canting over, her starboard gunwale almost under water, the cat swung round – and the moon came out, full and bright, bathing the scene.

'They're turning –' Carrick flung the words, pointing astern. The catamaran seen, the deception understood, the *Emma-Dee* came pivoting round less than half a mile away and her engines rose to full thrust. Her spotlight flared to life, the blast of an automatic rifle flamed from beside her wheelhouse, and a ragged line of holes stitched their way across the mainsail's inner edge.

'Damn that for a caper!' MacKenna scrambled down into the cabin and reappeared within seconds clutching an old Remington deer rifle. He wedged himself against the cockpit rail and pumped two shots at their pursuers. The third trigger pressure brought an empty click and he cursed. 'Jammed – aye, and they're gaining. Can't we go faster?'

Arran eyed the straining sails and shook her head. 'No. We should be reefing in as it is – we're risking turning her over.' The cat shuddered under the slamming blow of another sea, and water drenched aboard. 'Why have they stopped firing?'

'Saving it,' yelled Carrick. 'They know they've got us.' He glanced around. They were running fast, tacking to windward along the north shore of Nettri Island, the *Emma-Dee* now thundering less than a quarter mile astern, the wind and seas breaking over the cat's port hull and the gap steadily closing.

'If we could go in and beach her –' Arran pointed towards the shore. But the long black streak of high cliff-face revealed no break in its length, no chance of escape, a fury of broken water showing the rocks which fringed its base.

'There's another way.' MacKenna, the rifle discarded, pushed between them. 'Girl, if you had the spinnaker up and were heading for the cliffs how long would it hold?'

'Minutes, but –'

Carrick stared at them. 'We'd never make the shore, you know that.'

'Aye, and we're not going to try,' growled MacKenna. 'Arran, this contraption has retractable keel-boards, hasn't it?'

'Dagger-boards – there's a central hand-winch, beside the engine mounting. Why?'

'I'll show you.' A wild grin on his face, the old fisherman spurred them on. 'Carrick, they're engine-sailors like you. But maybe they don't know what happens when a wind meets a cliff, and we'll draw less than eighteen inches of water when those boards come up.' He glared at his daughter. 'Damn it, girl, get that helm down – now! Carrick, I want that spinnaker!'

They obeyed, still bewildered. Swinging round, the spinnaker blossoming, the wind almost dead astern, the *Gooshgash's* speed through the water rose to a bucking, tossing rush. Behind them, the motor-boat's path changed too, cutting to meet them on an inside angle, gaining several yards. The stutter of the automatic rifle sounded again, and the harsh spat of bullets smashing against the stern showed its user's aim was improving.

Carrick knelt down beside Clapper Bell, wadding a towel he'd pulled from a locker. He pressed it against the bo'sun's bloodsoaked thigh. 'Keep it there for now.'

'Right.' Bell bit back a groan as the deck heaved. 'What ... what's the old fellow tryin'?'

181

'Up with those dagger-boards!' MacKenna's shout tore Carrick away. He grabbed the handle and began cranking, feeling the pulley blocks turning as their cables dragged the two slim keel-boards up into the hull, boards without which the cat lost all chance of manoeuvring against the wind. MacKenna stood beside his daughter, peering ahead, ignoring everything but the sea ahead.

Carrick looked at the turmoil of water they were heading for, the way the cliff-face now towered high above them, the speed at which they were growing nearer, and knew a sudden grip of helpless panic. He fought it down, looked astern, and saw the motor-boat still pressing closer, coming in to make sure of her kill. Back there, Perris and Tenford must be exultant, sure they had only to press a little longer and force the catamaran to smash and break on the nearing rocks.

'Wait now,' shouted MacKenna in his daughter's ear. 'Wait for the wind – when it feels the cliff it'll run parallel.'

A grating quiver ran through the yacht as her starboard hull scraped an unseen rock, but she didn't slow – and Carrick's hope flared to life. The *Emma-Dee* was still coming on, relying on the manoeuvring power of her engines, gloating for the kill.

Above their heads, the spinnaker quivered. A ripple ran through the mainsail, then a shudder.

'Now!' barked MacKenna.

Arran swept the helm round. The *Gooshgash* hardly needed it. Sails lashing, her boom jerking then flying over their heads to slam to full travel of its reach, she was completely in the power of the wind – and that howling fury, its way barred by the cliff-face, was sweeping at a sudden right-angle. The catamaran skated round, swept on her new course like a paper bag, her crew hurled from their feet by the lurching turn, her sails striving to tear themselves loose.

Carrick picked himself up and looked astern. The *Emma-Dee* was turning, slowing, her engines screaming on full reverse pitch. For a moment the motor-boat wallowed in the trough of a clashing wave-pattern, then her whole length seemed to shake, the spotlight's beam flew wild. The sickening rip of her hull against the unseen rocks came loud above the elements.

Slowly, steadily, her bow rose clear – until the next shore-seeking breaker lifted her bodily and turned her over. There was a different sound, like a steel gouge raking through tin, a high-pitched shriek as her propeller shaft raced free.

And then the light had gone out and the *Emma-Dee* was still rolling over on her beam, rolling over and over . . .

'Poor baskets.' Clapper Bell was the first to find words, drawing himself painfully upright, staring as the motor-boat was blotted out in a white fury of breaking waves and the moon clouded over, as if in elemental sympathy.

A harsh, tearing bang and a wild flapping of falling sail jerked them back to their own problems. The spinnaker had burst loose, its nylon balloon flailing ahead like some giant streamer. As they cut it loose, it rose into the air and was swept away into the night.

It took long minutes to get the *Gooshgash* back under control. They rigged a tiny storm jib, dropped the daggerboards, and reefed the mainsail tight in. The cat handled sluggishly as Arran tried a sweeping curve of a tack to bring them up and round again. Her father seized the helm from her exhausted grip while Carrick found the answer. Water was already swirling around the cabin floor below, pouring in from the starboard hull.

'That rock we grazed,' grunted MacKenna. 'Well, this thing's got pumps, hasn't it?'

Arran nodded, thumbed a button, and the electric pumps began their chattering whine. They wallowed back through the heaving swell, the pumps slowing the inrush until it became a barely perceptible rise, until Carrick gauged they'd reached their goal. Grim-faced, he fired another of the yacht's rocket flares. It burst high – and its blossoming light showed a scene of horror.

The *Emma-Dee*, her back broken, was jammed on a reef of rock about fifty yards from the foot of the cliffs. Each sea which smashed against her widened the gap between bow and stern section. Stony-faced, Carrick fired a second flare as the first died down – and heard the girl by his side catch her breath as, bursting lower, the fresh light showed a fuller horror. A hand was waving desperately from the smashed frame of the motor-boat's wheelhouse, another man clung spread-eagled to the hatch cover of the bow section.

'We've got to do something,' she pleaded.

'We can't,' said her father grimly. 'Not in among that stuff. We've let them know we're here, but that's it.'

Another wave crashed over the *Emma-Dee*. The bow heaved and rolled over, vanishing with its human cargo. Next moment the flare sputtered out, giving them a last, fading glimpse of that wildly waving arm and the broken water which lay between.

A single storm-jib keeping her head into the wind, using the outboard to hold her position, the *Gooshgash* kept her vigil. Every three minutes Carrick fired one of the remaining rocket flares, while the pumps fought a slowly losing battle beneath his feet. He had two rockets left when an answering flare burst in the sky to the north. *Marlin* had arrived. Soon, to emphasize the fact, her big twenty-one-inch searchlights pierced the darkness and homed on the scene.

Diesels throttled back, deck-lights blazing, handled with superb precision, the grey bulk of the fishery cruiser moved in until the catamaran was sheltered close under her lee.

'You don't look too secure, mister,' bellowed Captain Shannon over the bridge loud-hailer.

Carrick cupped his hands and shouted back. 'She won't last long – but there's still a man in that wreck.'

184

'I'm not blind,' rasped Shannon's voice. 'But we'll get you aboard first.'

A brief bustle of activity broke loose on the *Marlin's* deck. A heavy boarding net and fenders were quickly draped over her side, a trio of seamen swarming part-way down while the yacht rose and fell below them. The two craft bumped together, and Clapper Bell was the first to be seized and hauled up the net to safety. Arran went next, then MacKenna, and finally, after a brief scramble to the cat's pulpit to knock loose the winch brake and let the anchor run out, Carrick jumped for the waiting mesh and climbed up on his own.

Captain Shannon was waiting, his round face grim. 'Stage one, mister. I've sent the others below – you'd better stay and see this through.'

Jumbo Wills was in charge of the breeches buoy party, with the line-firing gun set up aft of the bridge deck and both searchlights now trained on the stern half of the *Emma-Dee*. The line-gun's first shot was caught by the wind and fell wide. The second mate swore, sighted carefully, and tried again. The line ran clean and fell across the wreck's stern. They saw a figure leave the shelter of the wheelhouse, then dive back again as another breaker smashed down. When it cleared, they could see him still waiting in the shelter but the line had washed away.

'Third time lucky, Jumbo,' muttered Carrick, standing close beside him.

'It better be,' said Wills savagely. The line-gun was ready again, and this time he took an infinite care, firing on the peak of *Marlin's* roll.

The thin tongue of cord whipped out and fell straight across the wheelhouse roof. They saw the man reach out, grab it, and haul it in.

'Who is it, mister?' demanded Shannon from their rear.

'It could be Tenford – I'm not sure, sir,' Carrick told him. He heard Shannon growl, but if the Devil and his assorted apprentices had been out there the Superintendent of Fisheries would still have kept on trying.

The line secured, the rest followed quickly. First, a thicker line was run out, hauled in rapidly by the man in the wheelhouse. On its end went the breeches buoy hawser and block, a heavy pull for one man but a pull which held a promise of life. Agonizing minutes passed before it was across and the *Emma-Dee's* survivor had secured it to the main frame of the wheelhouse.

'Let her go,' snapped Jumbo Wills.

The canvas harness crossed the gap in a rattle of well-greased pulleys. Half a dozen of *Marlin's* burliest ratings stood ready while, at the other end, half-hidden by dashing spray, the figure by the wheelhouse fitted himself into the harness and finally gave a feeble signal.

'And haul –' Jumbo Wills swept his hand down and the breeches team began to heave. The man in the harness was lifted smoothly from the deck as the pulleys turned, his feet dangling just above the hungry wavetops, his whole body sometimes cloaked in a haze of spume.

'Steady –' The sudden rasp in Shannon's voice was their first warning, and they needed no further. Heading in towards the fishery cruiser, the great wave, nurtured somewhere out in the broad Atlantic, sweeping in towards its destiny, gathered the fishery cruiser up like a cork, sent a rolling shudder through its length, and passed on. Carrick had a brief impression of the same wave engulfing the man in the breeches buoy, of his reappearing, and then the wall of water hit the remains of the *Emma-Dee*. The thunder of its impact blended with a pistol-like snapping of wood and grate of metal as the motor-boat's stern section broke up.

The breeches hawser went slack, the man on its traverse disappeared.

'Haul away – double-quick!' Jumbo Wills winced as he snapped the order. The man in that canvas harness would

186

be dragged and buffeted over rock, slammed by waves, must already be halfway drowned.

Quickly, the water-soaked rope began to pile on deck as the breeches team slaved at their task. But it was still close to a minute before the breeches harness and its occupant rose dripping from the water, bumped briefly against *Marlin's* side, and were hauled aboard.

The battered form lay limp. Carrick bent over him, turned the face towards the light, and whistled. It was Tenford all right – a Tenford gashed and bleeding and barely conscious.

'You men get him below,' growled Shannon. 'Use the spare cabin next to the sick-bay.' As the seamen obeyed, he turned to Carrick. 'Seen your catamaran?'

Carrick nodded. The *Gooshgash* was settling fast, her ragged storm jib still fluttering. But with a little luck and if the anchor held there might be a chance to salvage her later.

'Second mate –' Shannon thumbed from Wills towards the bridge – 'take us out of this lot. As for you, Carrick, get changed into something dry – that's an order. Better use Wills's cabin. I gave the girl yours.'

The dry warmth 'tween decks seemed a luxury on its own as Carrick towelled himself down in Jumbo Wills's quarters then helped himself to a sweater, slacks and other items from the second mate's wardrobe. By the time he'd finished, *Marlin's* engines were slowing again. He looked out of the porthole and saw that she'd moved round to the lee of Abbot's Isle and was lying in calmer water.

He made his first call the sick-bay. Clapper Bell was lying comfortably in the hospital-type cot, with the wardroom steward in close, grinning attendance.

'How is he?' asked Carrick.

'Fine, according to the Old Man, sir,' said the steward. 'The bullet's still in him, but it missed the bone.'

Carrick accepted the diagnosis. On the fishery squadron, with no space for sea-going medical staff, every officer had to be qualified in advanced first-aid. He moved closer and sniffed Clapper Bell's breath. It reeked of straight navy rum.

'Captain's orders,' said the bo'sun dreamily. 'Good for all manner o' ills. Ach, what's a wee hole in the leg anyway?'

'Worth a month's shore leave, for a start,' suggested Carrick.

'Compensations, compensations.' Bell chuckled then threw a glare at the steward. 'I'm still waitin' for some food.'

'Not till you've seen a doctor,' countered the steward determinedly.

'I'm bo'sun of this ship –'

'And I run this sick-bay –'

He left them arguing and went along to the spare cabin. The door was open, and Captain Shannon was inside, standing a pace or two away from Tenford's bunk.

'He's conscious,' said Shannon quietly. 'But he won't last. Those rocks we dragged him over did the job – smashed most of his rib-cage, and at a guess there's massive internal haemorrhaging. I've given him morphia, for whatever good it can do.'

'Has he spoken, sir?'

'A little.' The Superintendent of Fisheries gave a heavy-shouldered shrug. 'We'd better get on with it. Time's running out.'

Carrick leaned over the bunk. Something approaching a smile twisted on Tenford's pallid face as he saw him. 'You – that was a pretty smart trick, Carrick. I – I should have known.'

'It was Sawny's idea.' Carrick glanced at Shannon and saw him nod. 'What happened to Doctor Perris?'

'That first wave –' Tenford gasped for breath. 'He went overboard. Then the rest – one by one.'

'Tenford –' Carrick hesitated.

The man nodded. 'I know. Perforated lungs – I'm drowning in – in my own way.'

'What happened to the bank boat's crew?'

'Dead, all of them.' The pain-bright eyes fixed on Shannon's face. 'Sorry about . . . about the boy, Shannon. I wasn't there. Perris and the other three . . . they'd gone to collect a load from Nettri on the *Emma-Dee*. The *Thrift* was there. She . . . she'd picked up that fool MacPherson floating on a hatch-cover, then ran in for shelter. Then they'd discovered the storeshed. Perris . . . Perris lost his head. He killed them on the boat, all except MacPherson. He saved . . . saved him for later.'

'We'd guessed most of it,' said Carrick softly. He heard Shannon give a long sigh, and knew the next thing he had to ask. 'Where did he – well, dispose of them?'

'They're buried in the old churchyard on . . . on Abbot's Isle.' Tenford gave a feeble shake of his head. 'Perris thought it was one place they'd never . . . never be found.' He mustered his last reserves of strength. 'That nephew of yours, Captain – he threw the safe keys overboard. That's why they didn't get the money. Then . . . then they took the *Thrift* out, to scuttle her well clear of the place. Perris bungled again . . . they'd spotted that damned catamaran sailing around and . . . and he was scared it might come back. He didn't wait to see the *Thrift* go down.'

'And the marijuana?' urged Carrick. 'You usually sent it out through Mallaig, right?'

'By rail to London, as boxed bulbs. Plenty . . . plenty of buyers.'

Carrick nodded. That part they could leave to the police. Chief Inspector Dawe was going to find some interesting follow-ups among the rail despatch records.

'Carrick –' Tenford wheezed and coughed, a slow trickle of blood running from one corner of his mouth. 'What about Johnny . . . Johnny Page and the girl?'

'They're fine.'

Tenford forced a smile. 'Thought so when . . . when there was no signal. Good.'

Shannon edged his way forward. 'Why do it, Tenford? Why start the whole filthy business with this devil's weed?'

'Money . . .' the man's voice was little more than a whisper. 'I got the island, but . . . but no money. Perris had the idea two years back. I . . . I had the contacts.' His eyes closed, then opened again. 'Captain, what . . . what happens now?'

Shannon gave a slow, deliberate shake of his head.

It was the last thing Robert Tenford would ever see. The rasping breathing stopped and his head fell back.

'That's it, mister.' Shannon checked that the pulse had stopped then pulled the top of the sheet over Tenford's face. Carrick followed him out of the cabin and closed the door.

'He threw the keys over –' Shannon muttered the words almost to himself. He stood silent for a moment then noisily cleared his throat. 'Like I said, that's it. I'm setting course for Mallaig. Once we've got Bell ashore and in hospital we can start tidying up the rest.'

'Sir?' Carrick raised an eyebrow.

Shannon nodded. 'The living and the dead, mister. We'd better tell the MacKennas what we're doing. You know where the girl is. Her father's on my bridge, acting like he owned the North Atlantic. I'll take care of him.' The prospect seemed to cheer him a little. 'Oh, and one other thing. I'll have to put you on Kenbeg for a few days to sort matters at that end. Any objections?'

'No, sir.' Carrick fought down a grin.

'I thought not.' Shannon gave a cynical sniff.

He went along the companionway, tapped on the door of his cabin, and it opened.

Arran MacKenna wore one of his white shirts, open at the neck, and a pair of borrowed khaki drill slacks, tightly belted round her waist. Her feet were bare and her hair, still damp, was combed back from her face then gathered in two short, schoolgirl-like pigtails.

She looked at him quietly for a moment then stood back, her grey eyes warm and waiting.

The deck-plates beneath their feet began to vibrate. *Marlin* was getting under way. Carrick closed the door, crossed to the intercom phone, and carefully took the receiver off its hook.

Then he turned, and she came into his arms.